CASSEROLE PARADE

by

Lorraine M. Harris

PublishAmerica
Baltimore

ISBN: 1-4241-6486-9
PUBLISHED BY PUBLISHAMERICA, LLLP
www.publishamerica.com
Baltimore

Printed in the United States of America

Dedication

To my husband, Lamont, and my two daughters, Nicole and Natalie. They love me unconditionally and encouraged me to realize my dream. I could not have done it without their prayers, encouragement, and advice. They are my inspiration.

Acknowledgement

I would love to list, by name, every person who continues to support me but the list would be too long and I'm sure I would miss someone. You know who you are! Please know that I appreciate and thank all my relatives and friends who continue to read and enjoy my books.

CHAPTER 1

Lisa Henderson's daily routine was to sit on her enclosed lanai, drink a cup of herbal tea and read the morning newspaper. As she glanced through different sections of the paper, her eyes were drawn to the obituaries. Was it instinct or curiosity?

Recently, she had moved to The Villages, a retirement community located in central Florida. Since she knew very few residents, she would have been surprised to recognize someone's name.

Regardless of the reason why she had read the obituary, she was pulling into the Little Baptist Church parking lot to attend a funeral service. Timidly, she entered the church.

It was almost full to capacity. Lisa's eyes darted to the left to the right, trying to locate an empty seat.

"Excuse me. I'm sorry. Please excuse me." Lisa climbed over people's feet as she made her way to the seat. Once she sat down, she drew in a deep breath and exhaled through her nose. She tilted her head slightly to the left and to the right she didn't see a familiar face.

Lisa was uneasy as she began to think how she would answer the question of how she knew Denise Tillman. With a tissue, she dabbed at the tiny beads of perspiration that had formed above her upper lip.

To calm her nerves, she turned her attention to the program she had been handed when she entered the church. Silently, she read. Denise Tillman was born and educated in Virginia. She had been married for thirty years to Joseph Tillman. No children were mentioned but the names of five nieces and three nephews were listed.

As Lisa continued to read, her ears perked up as she eavesdropped on the conversation the woman sitting next to her was having about Denise Tillman. Carefully, Lisa dropped the program she was holding. Slowly, she picked it up and eased her body closer to the woman.

"I have to say I was shocked. The news about Denise's death shook every core of my body. I just talked to her. Did you know she had cancer?"

The other woman answered, "No, I hadn't heard."

"Well, when I talked to Denise, she said the doctor was optimistic about treating the cancer. In fact…"

The woman halted her words in mid-sentence. She rolled her eyes at Lisa. Quickly, Lisa lowered her eyes, opened her purse and began rifling through it, as if she were looking for something.

The woman twisted her body but was unsuccessful in moving away from Lisa. The woman turned her back slightly away from Lisa but not before she gave Lisa a fierce, disgusted look. She leaned into the other woman and whispered.

"Well, at least she's no longer suffering."

The other woman shook her head. "You're right, but poor Joe. You know he doesn't cook. I'm not sure what he's going to do about eating."

"Pleaseee," the woman responded and threw up her hands in disgust. "There are what…" she shrugged her shoulders, "…at least twenty or so restaurants and country clubs serving food in The Villages. He can eat out every day of the week."

"Come on, no one wants to eat out every day. That gets old."

"Really! Is that why you eat out almost every meal?" They both laughed but covered their mouths with their hands to conceal the outbursts.

Both women cleared their throat. One of the women said, "The service is about to begin."

Lisa turned her attention to the man who was speaking. As she listened to the man's dismal demeanor, she prayed the service would become more upbeat. To tune out the lackluster voice, Lisa's mind began to wander.

CHAPTER 2

The fifty-five plus retirement community of The Villages provided Lisa with a lifestyle that was difficult to describe. Everything was on the premises and was accessible by a golf cart. The restaurants were unlimited, no country club fees or membership dues, swimming pools and recreational centers in every neighborhood, and live entertainment every day of the week.

With all of that, what could possibly be missing? For Lisa, the answer was male companionship.

To fill the void, she began seeking ways to meet single, eligible men to date. She joined the Christian Church Singles Club, read the local newspaper single ads, put her profile on the Internet, and signed up with a dating service. Inwardly, she chuckled as she recalled some of her dates.

Her first date came from the dating service. When Lisa opened the door, her date stood with a beautiful young woman by his side.

"Hello." He hurried on. "I hope you don't mind but my granddaughter will be our chauffeur for the night. I am no longer capable of driving a car."

Lisa didn't mind. Sitting in the back seat of the car was similar to riding in a chauffeured limousine. The date was going better than she had expected. The conversation was enjoyable and her date was quite interesting. Then their meals arrived.

"I probably should have mentioned it but since my stroke, I need you to cut up my food, as well as feed me."

Lisa tried to hide her surprise but she had not expected such a request. He never called her again.

Her second date was with a man who was ninety-one. He was extremely witty, did not look his age, and was charming. She wasn't bothered by his age but it was his reason why he was dating.

"I'm not getting any younger. So that I don't waste your time, I want you to know that I'm looking for a wife. I would prefer a younger woman so that in the event that I become ill, she will be able to care for me."

The last thing Lisa wanted was a husband and one that might make her a widow. Immediately, she revised her profile as to the age of the men she wanted to date.

Answering the newspaper ads, Lisa went out on a few dates, but those dates weren't much better. She didn't care about a man's height or attractiveness but she had little tolerance for deceitfulness. One man stated he was nearly six feet tall. When he arrived for their date, the man could not have been more than five feet tall as he peered up at her.

Another man sent her his picture and he had a beautiful, full head of brown hair. When she met him she could not keep her eyes off the toupee he wore. It reminded her of a cat that was curled up, sleeping. At times, she was tempted to pet or feed it.

The church group had twelve women and three men. The men that were in the group were like prime land up for auction. It was upsetting to Lisa to watch the women bid for the men's attention.

Accidentally, Lisa overheard the three men's conversation and opted out the group. She would never forget their words.

The man who was the most attractive and the youngest of the group stated, "I feel as though I have died and went to heaven. It's like having my own private harem."

The second man had traveled all over the world and was the most interesting. He said, "I know what you mean. I've never had so many choices but I feel guilty about dating five women at the same time."

The last man was on oxygen and wheezed as he spoke. He winked at the other men and stated. "I had to start taking the little blue pill."

Lisa jumped as something hit her foot and she was brought back to reality. When she turned her attention to the podium, a tall, slender built man was speaking. He had the deepest dimples with his curly brown hair mixed with specks of gray. At first she had no idea who the man was until he started talking lovingly about this wife, Denise.

The church and gravesite services had lasted about two hours. Everyone had been invited back to the Tillman's house for refreshments.

Easily, Lisa mingled with the Tillman's relatives and friends. She moved from one conversation to the other, listening but adding nothing. To her surprise, no one asked how she knew Denise or Joseph.

Lisa listened to a few more conversations and realized she had learned all there was to know about Joseph Tillman. He played softball, enjoyed going to the movies, and everyone fixated on the fact that he had little or no cooking skills.

Lisa decided to leave. Her feet were hurting, her stomach growling, and she had received the information she wanted to know.

CHAPTER 3

As Kellie Olson repositioned herself in the bed, a sharp pain went from her head to the back of her neck. Opening her eyes, she encountered a dull ache above her right eye.

Although she wasn't superstitious, she did pay attention to her intuition. At the moment, her gut was saying that this was not going to be a run of the mill type of day.

To top everything off, Roger, her husband, was still asleep. Rather than wake him, she eased out of bed and took a shower. After she dressed, she couldn't believe it. Roger was still sleeping.

Gently, she shook him. "Roger. Roger." He was not responding. She touched his pulse. It was slow and his breathing was shallow.

Immediately, she dialed 911. In less than ten minutes, the EMTs arrived. With efficiency, they took Roger's vitals, hooked him up to an IV, and determined that he would have to be transferred to the Leesburg Regional Medical Center.

While Roger was ushered off to an emergency examination room, Kellie sat in the waiting room. She passed the time by aimlessly flipping through outdated magazines and occasionally watching the low murmuring, wall mounted TV.

The time seemed to be in slow motion. Every time the door opened, she waited to hear her name called. As she stood to fix herself a cup of coffee, her wish had been answered.

"Mrs. Olson."

Quickly, Kellie responded. "I'm Mrs. Olson."

"Let's step outside."

Kellie listened closely to what the doctor was saying. "Mrs. Olson, from the initial examination and tests, your husband has had another stroke. I've ordered some additional tests. Based on the results, I will be able to provide you with a better assessment regarding the severity of the stroke and rehabilitation."

Kellie cracked open her front door and peeped out. The neighborhood was relatively quiet for it to be eight o'clock in the morning. As she stepped out the door, she shut and locked it. She glanced around and didn't see a single person walking a dog, riding a bicycle, or taking a walk.

Slowly, she peered over her shoulder. Her actions were as if she were a thief about to be caught.

If only she could park her car in the garage. It would only take her a few hours a day to unpack the boxes and identify the items she was giving to charity.

The last thing she wanted was to see a neighbor or for one of them to spot her. They were extremely caring and helpful but at times they could be a tad too inquisitive. She knew she should be grateful because they had been extremely thoughtful and supportive since they learned that Roger was in the hospital.

Unlocking her car door, she stopped holding her breath. She had made it—no neighbors—no questions to answer. As she opened the car door, she cringed, hearing the all too familiar, cheery voice of Lisa Henderson.

"Good morning, Kellie."

Slowly, Kellie turned around and waved. Through gritted teeth, she spoke. "Good morning, Lisa."

Lisa was standing with her lanai door open. Kellie smiled but did not make a move toward her house.

Kellie thought, *Maybe, she'll get the hint.* Instead, she noticed Lisa had closed her lanai door and was walking across the lawn. When Kellie got into the car, Lisa halted in her tracks.

"You're up early. How's Roger," Lisa shouted.

"He's resting. He had a lot of tests yesterday. Today, I'm supposed to discuss the results with the doctor."

"Well, where are you going so early?"

Kellie blew out air before answering Lisa. She gripped the steering wheel and slowly but sternly, she replied, "Thanks for asking about Roger. I'll tell him that you asked about him."

"But, Kellie…I wanted to know…" Lisa watched Kellie drive off.

CHAPTER 4

As Kellie drove to the Regal Care Assistant Living Complex, she thought about how times had changed. Regal Care was nothing but a nursing home with a fancy name. It was as if the name was changed to protect the innocent. Or was the name to create an image more acceptable to the caregiver as well as the one being placed?

Kellie was no doctor but from Roger's twisted face, his inability to speak coherently, and his left side paralyzed, he would need months of rehabilitation. Being realistic, she knew she wasn't capable of caring for him.

Before they had moved to Florida, Kellie had obtained information about a variety of nursing homes. Regal Care was the one that she thought would best suit their needs.

Once they were living in Florida, she and Roger made numerous trips to Regal Care. Since Roger would not discuss Regal Care, she could never receive any type of confirmation from him about whether he would like living there if the decision ever had to be made.

The only rooms Kellie would consider were the single rooms that were spacious, similar to a hotel suite. The rooms were furnished with a bed, a sleep sofa, two chairs, desk, and a separate bathroom. In addition, Regal Care allowed personal furnishings and decorations. At an extra cost, televisions and radios were available.

Despite Regal Care's reputation and its ability to provide better than average accommodations, Kellie was concerned about possible neglect if Roger had to be placed there. She would make morning and evening visits and spend the occasion night. This would assure her two things—the staff was performing their duties such as bathing Roger daily, feeding him, changing the bed linens, and giving him rehabilitation.

When she inquired about placing Roger in Regal Care, there had been a waiting list. As if God was reassuring her about her decision, the director called her the day after Roger's stroke and informed her that several openings had become available.

After Kellie parked her car, she sat and thought about her decision. She had mixed emotions about what she was about to do but she had no other options. She cleared her throat and willed herself not to cry.

The Director greeted Kellie and extended her hand. "Good morning, Mrs. Olson, and welcome to Regal Care. I know you've visited Regal Care on numerous occasions but I still want to give you a quick tour."

Regal Care had not changed since Kellie's last guided tour. As she had remembered, Regal Care had everything on the premises. The staff seemed to work efficiently. It was staffed with a 24/7 doctor, registered nurses, nursing assistants, and volunteers.

The facility had a large dining room, as well as smaller eating rooms, an exercise and rehabilitation room, library, and game room. If Roger's doctor requested special medical care, arrangements would be made to accommodate the need. The tour alleviated Kellie's concerns and reinforced her decision.

After the paperwork was completed, the decision was final.

CHAPTER 5

When Kellie arrived at the hospital, she was told that Roger was having some tests performed. Since his room was being cleaned, she walked down the corridor to the waiting room.

Kellie opened the door and noticed four people sitting in different corners of the room. A couple was holding hands. She thought they were probably husband and wife. The other two people were women. One woman looked to be about Kellie's age. The other woman appeared to be in her early to late seventies. Before Kellie took a seat, she fixed a cup of coffee.

After glancing through several magazines she became uninterested. She turned her attention to the people in the waiting room. The couple was talking in low tones. The elderly woman was sitting with her eyes closed. The woman her age was staring straight ahead. For some unknown reason, Kellie strolled over to the woman.

"Excuse me, do you mind if I sit down beside you?"

The woman jumped slightly.

"I didn't mean to startle you. It's just that I have zero tolerance when it comes to waiting. My name is Kellie Olson. I'm here about my husband."

"Nice to meet you. My name is Amanda Roberts. I'm here for my husband too. He was brought in yesterday."

Amanda stopped and dabbed at the tears running down her cheeks. "My husband had a stroke."

"I'm sorry. My husband, Roger, has had numerous mini-strokes. It seems like each one gets worse. When all the tests are conducted, the doctor will determine his rehabilitation."

"I was told almost the same thing." They smiled at each other.

Kellie changed the subject. "Where do you live?"

"In The Villages."

"Me too."

"Have you been there long?"

"About five years." Amanda lowered her voice. "When we first moved to Florida, I hated it. But when we moved to The Villages, I…we knew we had found the retirement community for us."

"Yeah, I have to agree. There's so much to do. What types of things do you do?"

"Well, I'm still working."

"Oh. That's too bad. I thought maybe we could do something together sometime."

"That would have sounded fun several weeks ago, but with my husband having a stroke…" Amanda's voice trailed off.

"I understand, but why don't you take my card. You may want to talk to me about caring for your husband. This time, when my husband is released, I'm placing him in an assistant living facility."

"Oh…" Amanda tried to cover up her surprise to Kellie's statement. "You're not taking him home?"

"No. There's no way I can give him the type of care that he needs. Listen, it wasn't an easy decision but it's something I have to do."

Amanda heard herself say, "I understand."

Kellie patted Amanda's leg. "Listen, call me if you need information about nursing homes. I've researched them all. In addition, I belong to a support group. The members are women who married older men. We discuss everything from impotency to finances. You might want to attend one of the meetings."

Before the women could continue their conversation, the door opened. A nurse entered.

"Mrs. Roberts."

CHAPTER 6

Over the next several weeks, Lisa tried to put the idea of meeting Joseph Tillman out of her mind. However, it nagged at her every day. About six weeks after the funeral, she made a decision.

Lisa knew meeting Joseph Tillman was going to be easier than she originally thought. He didn't cook. Delivering him a casserole was her way of introducing herself to him.

And she had just the recipe. Her chicken and rice casserole was a dish that people could not eat enough of and everyone said that it was incredibly delicious. Making the casserole was easy; the hard part was delivering it.

Lisa pulled her car in front of the house and parked. She took a deep breath to ease her rapidly beating heart. The palms of her hands were sweaty and she was quivering.

For a minute, she thought about leaving but somehow she mustered up the courage and got out of the car. As she approached the house the casserole dish was hot to the touch. Carefully, she opened the unlocked lanai door.

Between the heat and Lisa's nervousness, she began to perspire. Afraid she would drop the dish she placed it carefully on a small table near the door. Then, she rang the doorbell.

Patiently, she waited. After pushing the doorbell button again, she peeped over her shoulder. She hoped none of his neighbors would see her.

After the third time of ringing the doorbell, she decided to leave. As she turned and was about to pick up the dish, she heard a deep, husky male voice.

"Hello, may I help you?"

Lisa turned around. Closely looking at Joseph Tillman, she thought he was more handsome than she remembered.

She knew she was staring a little too long. Taking her time, she thought about how to introduce herself. She wanted to sound sincere and genuine.

With a smile, she said, "My name is Lisa Henderson." She reached her hand out to shake his. "I was a friend of your wife…"

Before she could continue, Joseph cut her off. He shook his head. "Forgive me, but I didn't know all of Denise's friends. We had varied, separate interests. While I played softball, she was active playing cards, going to bingo, and volunteering at the church."

She grinned as she gave him a nod, letting him know she understood. She prayed he wouldn't ask her where and how she knew Denise. If he asked she would have to stretch the truth. The only commonality she had with his late wife was bingo.

Since she didn't want to lie, she quickly told him why she had made the visit. She picked up the casserole dish.

"I thought maybe you would enjoy eating something homemade."

Joseph responded with a chuckle. "Denise must have told every person she met that I didn't know how to cook."

"Well, at least when you weren't together, you know she talked about you." Nervously, Lisa sniggered.

She couldn't believe she had said that. She had to leave before she made a complete fool of herself.

Lisa thought, *Lord, please help me.*

Quickly, she broke the silence before it became awkward. Joseph had not taken the dish she had offered to him. Her hands were uncomfortable from the dish's heat. Again, she pushed the dish toward him.

"I hope you like casseroles."

"Like them. Are you kidding? This is a nice, welcomed surprise. I was about to go to Cracker Barrel. It's the closest food that I have found that taste homemade. So, you've saved me."

He paused and gave her a wide tooth smile. "I have an idea. Why don't you join me?"

"Oh I couldn't."

"Please. As much as I enjoy leftovers and hate the thought of not knowing what I'm going to eat from one meal to the next, I still prefer eating with someone."

Again, Lisa protested, but just enough not to appear eager. "Oh I don't know. I don't want to intrude."

"Please, I insist. Come in."

CHAPTER 7

Although Kellie was meeting with the doctor, she didn't have to be told about Roger's condition. The only question Kellie needed answered was what was the severity of the stroke?

"Mrs. Olson, your husband's stroke has caused permanent paralysis on his left side. I doubt if he'll regain any use of that side of his body."

"What about his speech?"

"I can't say unconditionally but I would say that your husband will require more speech therapy than before. His speech may be slurred but over all, there's no medical reason why he shouldn't talk. Do you have any other questions?"

"Yes I do. Have you talked to my husband and explained all of this to him?"

"Yes I did. He seemed to understand what I was telling him."

"Will I be able to take care of him at home?" Kellie already had made her decision but she wanted to hear it from a medical viewpoint.

"If you take him home, it's going to require a substantial amount of work on your part."

"Exactly how much work?"

"You'll have to bathe him, dress him, and possibly feed him. Being the caregiver is never easy. Most of all, you and your husband are going to have to be patient. As I stated earlier, this stroke was more debilitating than the other strokes he had."

When Kellie walked into Roger's room, his eyes were closed. She approached the bed and touched his arm. He opened his eyes.

"Hi, honey. How are you feeling?"

His facial expression was sullen. He said nothing. She patted his hand and smiled, indicating that she understood. She sat in the nearby chair. She chewed her lower lip, took a deep breath and began.

"Roger, I talked to the doctor about your stroke. He also mentioned that he talked to you. Did you understand what he told you?"

Slowly, he nodded his head. For a second Kellie looked at Roger but quickly lowered her eyes.

Nervously, she sat wringing her hands together. Although she didn't make direct contact with Roger, she couldn't avoid his scrutinizing expression.

"Roger, there is no easy way of saying this. As much as I love you, I'm not equipped to take care of you. Not this time."

Kellie paused and added. "I could hire a nurse but since the cost wouldn't be covered by our health insurance, it would be too expensive."

She waited and watched his reaction. His lips were pursed and his eyes were shut tightly.

Gently, she tugged at the hospital gown. He opened his eyes. "Do you remember the Regal Care Assistant Living Complex we looked at?"

Kellie wanted him to respond but he lowered his eyes. She couldn't tell if he had closed them or not.

"Well, that's where you'll stay until..." She almost added, *...until you're better.*

"Ar...are...you...g-g-g...going...t-t-t-to...live...th-th-th...there...t-t-too?"

"No, dear. I'm going to remain living in The Villages."

"Wh…wh…why?"

"Because Regal Care is for individuals who need help doing daily functions, like showering, dressing, and eating." She added with a smile, "And occasionally, I'll spend the night with you."

A frown covered Roger's face. His eyes watered. He raised his right hand and pointed a finger toward the door.

Kellie opened her mouth and then closed it. When she stood up, she leaned over to kiss him good-bye but he turned his head away. Tears leaked out the corner of her eyes. She stood beside the bed for a few moments, turned, and walked out.

Outside of Roger's room, she let out soft sobs.

While driving home, Kellie's mind was full of memories. When she married Roger he did not seem that much older than she. At the time, he was good-looking, healthy, and full of life.

After the death of his wife, a mutual friend introduced them. Six months later, they were married which raised quite a few eyebrows.

Despite what their friends and relatives predicted, their marriage had lasted longer than one year. In fact, Roger suffered his first stroke after they had been cruising to celebrate their tenth year wedding anniversary.

The stroke had left Roger using a walker but with rehab he regained his ability to walk on his own. But Kellie was reminded daily of his weakened condition. When he tired, he had a tendency to drag his left leg and he had difficulty speaking. From that time on, Kellie realized that Roger was never going to be the man she had originally married.

CHAPTER 8

Kellie was heartbroken thinking about Roger and how he reacted to being placed in Regal Care. But what options did she have? They couldn't afford the expense of a nurse and God knows she didn't have the skills, ability, or patience to take care of him at home.

She understood his disappointment but it was hard for her to accept his behavior. Since the discussion, Roger was treating her like she had a disease and he was afraid of catching it.

When she kissed and hugged him, he did not return the affection. In addition, he made no attempts to communicate with her. Despite his demeanor, Kellie continued to be loving, caring, and attentive.

This was the day Kellie had been dreading. Roger was leaving the hospital and moving into Regal Care.

To help the transition, Kellie had decorated his room with items from their home. The walls were adorned with two of his favorite art pieces and lots of framed pictures of the two of them, as well as friends.

Roger was being transported to Regal Care by ambulance. Kellie had taken care of the paperwork regarding his discharge therefore she was at Regal Care waiting for his arrival.

As Kellie glanced at the wall clock, she began pacing the floor. *Where's the ambulance? It should have been here.*

"Mrs. Olson."

Kellie spun around to find a green-clan uniform woman in her mid to late twenties standing at the door. She smiled at Kellie.

"Hi. "My name is Marcie Larson. I will be your husband's primary nurse. He also has a nursing assistant. I understand you already met Mrs. Gordon, the head nurse in charge."

Kellie nodded her head and reached her hand out and shook the woman's hand. "Hi. I'm Mrs. Olson."

Awkwardly, they stood as they inspected each other. Marcie broke the silence.

"Your husband should be arriving shortly. Sometimes, the discharge procedures take longer than expected. Can I get you a cup of hot coffee or tea while you wait?"

"Thanks but I'm fine. I'm just a little nervous…"

Kellie's voice trailed off. She wanted to share more but thought it was inappropriate to discuss her concerns with the staff.

"I understand, but he'll be fine."

As Marcie walked out the door, she spotted a stretcher being pushed in her direction. She peeped her head around the door and said, "I think your husband has arrived."

Kellie waited and within seconds, Roger was ushered into the room. She stepped out of the way as Roger was put in the bed.

It wasn't Roger's partially twisted face that caused Kellie to cringe. He had the most distasteful facial expression as he stared at her. Slightly, she turned. She didn't want anyone to see the threatening tears about to spill from her eyes.

"Mr. Olson, I'm Marcie Larson." She patted his hand and added. "I'll be taking good care of you." She tucked the sheets under Roger and smoothed the top cover before leaving.

When Marcie exited the room, Kellie approached Roger. As she bent over to kiss him, he turned his head.

"Roger, please. This is just as hard for me as it is for you." She tried to sound upbeat as she waved her hand around.

"When you close the door, you would think that you were at home." She pointed. "See I've decorated your room with your favorite paintings. Do you see all of our pictures and our friends' photos that I've brought? Not only that, your favorite reclining chair is situated by the window, you have a view of the courtyard."

After Kellie finished, she was disappointed. Instead of paying attention to her, he had turned his head toward an empty wall.

Kellie had planned to spend most of the day with Roger. She wanted to make the transitional move as pleasant as possible. Instead, she left, unable to cope with Roger's indifference toward her.

CHAPTER 9

As Kellie pulled her car into the driveway, she spotted Lisa sitting on her lanai. Out loud, Kellie said, "Does she ever go in the house?"

Laughing slightly, Kellie shook her head. She waved at Lisa as she closed the car door.

"Hi, Lisa."

"Hi, Kellie." Without hesitation, Lisa asked, "How's Roger doing?"

"He's doing as well as can be expected."

"Well, I would love to visit him."

"I think he would like that but why don't you wait a couple of weeks. He needs time to adjust to his new surroundings and routine."

"I understand. Well, let me know when I can visit him."

Lisa watched Kellie stroll into the house. Thoughts of her deceased husband, Paul, entered her mind.

She knew how difficult it could be to decide what to do about an ailing spouse. When Paul was diagnosed with cancer, Lisa had made some difficult decisions. Instead of placing Paul into a nursing home, she cared for him until he died. If she had to do it again, she might have made a different decision because she lived with constant feelings of frustration, loneliness, hopelessness, and powerlessness.

It was heartbreaking when Paul died but yet a blessing. His pain and suffering was over not only for him but also for her.

After Paul's death, Lisa worked until she was eligible to retire. Until her friend, Diane Benson moved to The Villages, Florida, Lisa had not thought about moving.

Lisa and Diane became friends when they worked together at the Maryland Gas Company. Lisa and Diane were one of the few female managers. Lisa was head of the Civil Rights Office and Diane was over Human Resources.

Diane invited Lisa to visit her and instantly, Lisa fell in love with The Villages. Without hesitation, she decided to move. Before she returned to Maryland, she put a down payment on a lot. However, she had to sell her house.

That was the easy part. What was causing her anguish was the thought of breaking the news to her two sisters.

Lisa decided to contact a real estate agent before talking to her sisters. She thought it would be easier. To Lisa's surprise, her house sold in less than forty-eight hours.

When Lisa's sisters, Alicia and Rachel, drove up to Lisa's house, they were stunned to see the *sold* realty sign. By the time Lisa opened the door to greet them, they were talking and asking questions at the same time, in high pitched tones.

"Alicia…Rachel…come in." They busted through the door and demanded answers.

Instead, Lisa ushered them into the dining room. The table was already set and the food was on the table.

"Why don't we sit down and eat lunch. Then I'll answer all your questions?" Reluctantly, they agreed. As they began to eat, Alicia could wait no longer.

"When did you decide to sell your house?"

Lisa's vocal cords tightened but she was able to utter her response, barely above a whisper. "When I decided to move to Florida."

CHAPTER 10

No one spoke for a noticeable length of time. But the expressions on her sisters' faces said it all. Rachel had tears shimmering in her eyes while Alicia had a disgusted, annoyed look.

Lisa broke the silence. "Look, I need a change." She paused but avoided making eye contact with her sisters.

Defensively, Lisa asked, "Why not move to Florida?"

Her sister Alicia stated firmly. "For one reason, all of your family is here. Besides, you don't know anyone in Florida."

"Yes, all my family is in Maryland, but I can visit any time I want. And I do know someone in Florida. Do you remember my friend, Diane Benson?"

Her sisters glanced at each other and shrugged.

"You remember Diane," urged Lisa.

"Oh, the crazy woman," said Alicia.

Lisa and Alicia locked eyes. "She's not crazy. She's unique and she's had a string of overwhelming situations she's had to face."

"Oh I remember her now. Isn't she the woman whose husband left her after twenty years of marriage? He was having an affair with a woman from their church."

"Yes, that's Diane."

"Did her husband marry the woman he was having an affair with?"

"Yes and they recently had a baby."

"You're kidding me. No wonder she's off balance."

Alicia and Rachel laughed. Lisa did not join them because there was no humor in what Diane had been through.

"Alicia! Rachel!" They turned their attention back to Lisa as she continued.

"Anyway, I'm moving to the same place where Diane lives."

Then Alicia asked, "You mean to tell me that you would rather live near a friend than family?"

"What is that supposed to mean?"

"I don't have to spell it out. You know exactly what I mean."

"No I don't." Anger spilled from Lisa's tone.

"Right, you have no idea what I'm talking about." Alicia threw up hands.

Rachel tried to play peacemaker. "Come on, Alicia and Lisa. Let's not get into an argument over this."

"I'm not arguing. I'm merely stating that we understand why she wants to move. Whether or not she wants to admit the truth is another matter," said Alicia with a slight edge to her voice.

Alicia continued and then demanded. "If I'm lying then tell us about this retirement place."

"It's a community near Orlando. It's called The Villages."

Alicia insisted, "Come on Lisa, don't be shy about it now. Tell us more."

Lisa stood up from the table and left Alicia and Rachel for a few minutes. When she returned, she invited them to join her in the family room.

"I have a videotape of where I'll be living. It will give you a better sense of why I've chosen The Villages," explained Lisa.

After the videotape ended, Alicia said, "I've made my point."

Rachel tried a different approach. "Hey, I have an idea. Why don't we live together?"

"That would be fun," said Lisa with enthusiasm. She saw the excitement in Rachel's eyes but added, "Rachel, I would still want to live in Florida. Would you?"

With sadness in her eyes, Rachel answered, "I was thinking we could sell our houses, buy one together, and live here in Maryland."

"I'm sorry. It was a good suggestion but I've made up my mind about Florida. Why don't you visit before you say no?"

With bitterness lacing Alicia's tone, she said, "Rachel don't be fooled by Lisa. The last place she wants to live is in Maryland and be around her family. Why do you think she never had children?"

Lisa couldn't believe her ears. *What made Alicia say that?* She never had children because she couldn't conceive. She and Paul tried adopting, infertility treatments, and considered a surrogate but their efforts had been unsuccessful. At age thirty, she spiraled into menopause that ended their hope of having children. Again, Rachel tried to smooth things over.

"Lisa, if this is what you want then I'm happy for you. Like you said, you can visit us any time."

Rachel stood up and gave her sister a reassuring hug. Alicia watched her sisters, shaking her head in disgust.

Under her breath, Alicia said, "You can sweep dirt under a rug but in time, it always creeps out."

CHAPTER 11

Moving to Florida had not been an easy decision for Lisa. However, her attitude about life was that everything happened for a reason. In addition, there was no decision that could not be reversed.

The primary reason Lisa was moving to The Villages was because of her friend Diane. The only concern Lisa had was that Diane would feel compelled to include her into her social activities such as card playing, bowling, or shopping.

Lisa didn't need nor did she want Diane to be her social director. She was an extrovert and when she visited The Villages, people were friendly and constantly struck up conversations. In addition, there were enough things to do that she would have no problem keeping busy.

At first, Lisa was considering building a new home, but decided to look at pre-owed houses. What a twist of fate when she found a house on the same street where Diane lived.

Lisa recalled the day she moved to The Villages. Diane was visiting her daughter in Maryland. With Diane away, Lisa was a little nervous. However, when the moving van pulled up to her patio villa, two women approached her.

"Hi. Welcome to The Villages," the two women spoke in unison.

"Hi and thank you both."

"You must be Diane's friend." The tall woman with short brown hair made the introductions.

"I'm Arlene Woodson." Then she turned to the woman standing beside her. "And this is Kellie Olson.

Lisa thought how attractive the woman was with the light green eyes and reddish brown hair. Not to mention her Barbie doll figure.

"You already know, my name is Lisa Henderson."

Kellie stated, "Yes Diane told us all about you. It seemed like every time you visited her, we were either away or not available to meet you. Well, here we are now."

"You know where Diane lives, three doors down from you." Arlene pointed to the house where stone landscaping had been substituted for all the grass.

"I live beside Kellie."

"I probably won't remember." Lisa laughed nervously.

Kellie gave her a tip. "First, it's important to learn which village you live in. If not, you might get lost."

Arlene pointed to her house and said, "After that you have to remember which house is yours. I have a flowerbed in front of my white picket fence. And Kellie has rose bushes in front of hers."

Kellie added, "With the villas looking similar in appearance, it's easy to drive into someone else's driveway. You might want to put some distinguishing marker or change your landscaping to distinguish your house from the others."

After the moving van unloaded the last box, Kellie suggested, "Why don't we help you unpack your boxes and anything else you want us to do?"

"Oh no. I couldn't impose on you like that."

"Impose, please. That's what neighbors are for. You'll find that in The Villages, your neighbors are more than happy to help you in any way they can."

Before they began unpacking boxes, Arlene made an observation. "Although you bought a resale, I see you've made some changes to the house."

"Just a few. Would you like to see what I did?"

"By all means," said Kellie. "Lead the way."

Lisa gave them a tour while explaining in detail, the changes she had made and why. "I lowered the breakfast bar to accommodate regular chairs for extra sitting when I entertain. I extended the patio, and reduced the kitchen in order to have the washing machine and dryer inside the house. I thought it would be too hot to do laundry in the garage."

"Thanks Lisa for showing us your house. But if we're going to help you then we better get started in unpacking these boxes," stated Kellie.

Working non-stop, except for water and potty breaks, the women completed their mission of helping Lisa. Glancing around her new surroundings, she smiled. She could not believe how much had been accomplished. Her kitchen had been organized; the bed made-up, and several pictures had been hung on the walls.

"Ladies, I appreciate all your help. I can finish the rest on my own." Hesitating for a moment, Lisa smiled.

"In exchange for helping me, let me fix dinner."

They protested but Lisa insisted. To their surprise, her idea of treating them to dinner was calling out for pizza.

"You'll fit right in," stated Arlene. They laughed.

CHAPTER 12

Arlene and Kellie moved to The Villages about the same time as Diane. That was about all Lisa knew about the two women. On the other hand, they seemed to know everything about her, putting her at a disadvantage. While they ate pizza, Lisa inquired.

"Why did you ladies move to The Villages?"

Arlene shared first. "I moved to The Villages from Pennsylvania. I have one daughter who went to college in San Diego, California. After graduation, she was offered a job, accepted it, and still lives there. Because of the distance, I see her about twice a year."

Arlene paused for a second. Her eyes turned sad and her facial expression seemed as if she had drifted to another place. Finally, she started talking again.

"When my daughter has a business trip to her company's Orlando office, she usually makes arrangements to visit me. I guess I could fly to California to see her, but since 9/11—I hate to fly. I'm sorry I'm digressing."

Kellie's voice was laced with annoyance. "Yes, please stay focused." She rolled her eyes as she thought inwardly, *I wish Arlene would hurry along.*

"My husband, Harold, and I moved here three months after we both retired from the Pennsylvania school system. He and I were principals. When we moved to The Villages, we were like two small children in an amusement park. We were thrilled with the active lifestyle and we enjoyed going to the dances, taking day bus trips, and basically trying anything new."

Arlene stopped and cleared her throat. "One evening when we were at the Arnold Palmer Legends Country Club having dinner, Harold—did I tell you his name?" She looked at Lisa and waited until she acknowledged.

"Well, before we ordered our meal, he said he didn't feel well…he never complained about anything…this was unusual for him. Anyway, one minute he was complaining about a pain and then without warning, he fell out of the chair." Arlene closed her eyes for a moment and slowly, shook her head.

"Harold had a massive heart attack and died before the paramedics arrived. I…we never expected…I mean…losing Harold…was heartbreaking. He was taken away from me too soon." Arlene used the back of her hand and wiped away a falling tear.

Her voice cracked as she continued. "To be truthful, I had no reason to live. Our retirement and growing old was supposed to be with the two of us. As far as I was concerned, my life had ended too. I was lost, angry, and empty." Lovingly, she smiled at Kellie.

"Thank God for my Villages' friends and neighbors. With Harold's unexpected death, I was glad I was living here."

"What about your daughter? Did you think about moving to California?" asked Lisa.

Shaking her head, Arlene stated, "It never crossed my mind. For one thing, my daughter's job requires her to travel at least two weeks out of the month. I would have been left alone most of the time. Besides, when I told my daughter that I was staying in The Villages, I could hear the relief in her voice."

"It might not seem like a lot, but Diane and Kellie made me do basic stuff like get out of the bed, shower, dress, and eat."

According to Arlene, Diane and Kellie had been her saving grace. Listening closely to Arlene, Lisa could not miss the love she had for them.

"They became my extended family. Although they included me in their social activities, I was never made to feel like a tag along—you know a third wheel."

In addition, Arlene explained how she appreciated the fact they never treated her husband's death as though it never happened. They did not tiptoe around their conversations and they allowed her to vent and cry when she needed it.

Arlene finished her story by saying. "If it weren't for me living in The Villages and having Diane and Kellie I'm not sure what would have happened to me."

CHAPTER 13

Kellie waited for several minutes to make sure that Arlene was finished. When she heard nothing else, she began sharing her story.

"My husband, Roger, is somewhat older than I am." She paused for a moment and raised her eyes upward.

"Before I retired, Roger had a stroke. I...we moved from the cold, wintry weather of Ohio to the Sunshine State."

A pessimistic grunt escaped from Kellie. "I always wanted to live in a warm climate. Roger on the other hand wanted no parts of the cancer causing sun. He also feared that the heat and humidity would be unbearable. You would have thought that with him being cold constantly he would have welcomed a warmer climate." Kellie glanced at Lisa who shrugged.

"Roger didn't want to move to Florida but once we visited The Villages, it didn't take much convincing. He liked the lifestyle. Although he never voiced it I think he wanted to make sure I would be comfortable if something happened to him."

Lisa nodded, reached for another piece of pizza and continued to listen.

"I love it here. If Roger were to die or if I had to place him in a nursing home, I wouldn't have a problem adjusting to being single."

Lisa lowered her head. Although she did not want to pass judgment, she was uncomfortable listening to Kellie discuss her future in the event of her husband's death. Lisa's expression did not miss Kellie's observing eye.

"You're probably thinking I'm rather cold, but I'm a practical person. I don't wait for things to happen. For example, I've already made plans for Roger in the event that he has another stroke and needs twenty-four hour care."

Lisa' mouth was agape. Quickly, she shut it and hoped Kellie did not notice her surprised reaction to her comment.

"I'm like a boy scout—be prepared. I located the most beautiful, well-staffed nursing home. I mean…the political correct name is assistant living facility. Roger and I visited the place together."

Lisa was curious. "What was his reaction?"

"Uh…he didn't say much but I could tell he was impressed with the overall appearance, staffing, and décor.

Arlene exhaled noisily. "Come on, Kellie, be truthful. How would you react if Roger had taken you to a nursing home?"

Kellie was surprised at Arlene's statement. "I would embrace it. Why should Roger have to take care of me if I can't function for myself?"

Arlene didn't respond.

"Well?"

"Kellie, we've had this discussion before and as you know, we do not see eye to eye on this subject. So let's agree to disagree."

"What do you think Lisa?"

"Uh…uh." Lisa was stammering. She didn't want to be brought into this discussion.

Kellie was persistent. "Lisa, what do you think?"

"Well…in my opinion, everyone has to make their decision based on their particular situation. I don't think there's a right or wrong decision when it comes to caring for someone."

"Boy, didn't you dodge a bullet? Talk about being politically correct."

Lisa started to say something but changed her mind. "Well, ladies, I'm really tired and I have a long list of things to take care of tomorrow. So, if you don't mind, I'd like to call it a day."

CHAPTER 14

After Lisa's move-in day, a friendship had been bonded among she, Arlene, and Kellie. While Diane was away, the women took Lisa under their wings.

To acquaint Lisa with The Villages and the surrounding areas, Kellie and Arlene planned an outing everyday for Lisa.

As Arlene put it, "Girl, it's a necessity for you to know the best places to shop, as well as eat."

They drove to the indoor malls at Leesburg, Ocala, and Orlando. When they drove to Wildwood, Kellie was quick to explain.

"Wildwood has a quaint, small town appearance but the shopping and eating is limited," But there is one surprise—the bakery.

Within The Villages, the shopping was located primarily on the two town squares. Nightly, they went to the various restaurants and country clubs, the Church-on-the Square for concerts, and to the town squares for happy hour, socializing, and dancing.

By the time Diane returned, Lisa had settled into a routine and was maneuvering around The Villages as if she had lived there for years.

With the cost of gas sky rocketing, Arlene and Kellie convinced Lisa to buy an electric golf cart. They assured her that she would conserve energy as well as save money.

Arlene said, "I use my golf cart as much as possible. Since many of the stores, activities and medical facilities are on the premises, you'll be able to reach them by golf cart."

In addition, she had begun to make friends. As she participated in playing cards, joined the wellness center, and was learning how to line dance, she met an array of people. Regardless of where she went people were not shy in making introductions and striking up conversations.

Commenting to Diane, Arlene, and Kellie, she stated. "I cannot remember a place where I have met so many friendly people."

Quickly, Arlene added, "That's why The Villages is known as, "The friendliest hometown."

Making friends was the easy part. Lisa discovered the difficulty was in balancing time to be with friends, participating in things she enjoyed, and doing household chores. Actually, she discovered there weren't enough hours in the day to do everything.

Now she understood what people meant when they shared. *"When you live in The Villages, retirement is like having a job."*

Regardless of how much she enjoyed her new friends and the fun, there were times when she needed to vegetate—to do nothing but relax, read, watch television, or do household chores.

In an effort to make the time she needed, she learned to draw her shades, park her car in the garage, and keep her garage door down. Most neighbors and friends assumed she wasn't home.

If she did not take measures to plan for "me time," some of her neighbors and friends had a tendency to drop in unannounced. It wasn't the unexpected visits that bothered her, but it was their persistent attitude. They made her feel guilty or applied an unusual amount of peer pressure.

Constantly, she was asked, *"What are you doing that you can't do tomorrow?"* Or they would state, *"Come out and play any way. Chores can always be done another day."*

At times, Lisa was overwhelmed living in The Villages, as she tried to do too much. Wanting to become physically fit, she started walking, swimming, playing tennis, and riding her bicycle. Then, she took golf lessons and learned how to play a game similar to tennis, called pickle ball. In addition to doing the physical activities, she played cards, made photo scrapbooks, and attended various recreation center sponsored events.

As hard as it was to say "no" to her friends and neighbors, it was necessary. In addition, with her new quest to find eligible men to date, she only had so much time.

CHAPTER 15

The casseroles Lisa delivered were mostly accepted with a welcomed smile and open arms. Usually, the men were excited to have the opportunity to receive a home cooked meal as well as have someone to share it with.

The exception to the rule was Mr. Marvin T. Adams. Thinking back to that day, Lisa could laugh now. At the time, it scared her enough to rethink whether she wanted to continue taking casseroles to grieving widowers. Marvin Adams's daughter would be etched in her memory forever.

When Lisa read the obituary of Pauline Adams, she had not recalled the mention of children. Generally, the rule for children was that they were gone after about six weeks.

However, when Lisa arrived at Marvin's house with a casserole, a young woman answered the door. She was perhaps in her late thirties or forties. When the woman greeted Lisa, her facial expression and body language was intimidating.

As sweetly as possible, Lisa spoke. "Hi, my name is Lisa Henderson. Is Mr. Adams at home?"

Before the woman answered, Lisa was trembling. She thought the woman was human, but she reminded her of a dog about to attack. The woman growled and snarled as if protecting her territory.

"My name is Nanette Adams. May I ask who you are?"

"A f-f-f-friend...I m-m-mean a n-n-neighbor." Lisa was stuttering and beads of sweat were forming on her upper lip and forehead.

"Mr. Adams is my father. Why do you want to see him?"

Before Lisa could answer, the young woman closed the door gently and joined her on the lanai. She stepped too close to Lisa. She was having difficulty breathing. It was as if the young woman had sucked all the oxygen out of the small-confided space.

Nanette was acting similar to a well-trained guard dog as she circled Lisa and sniffed at her, trying to determine whether she was friend or foe. After Nanette finished her inspection, she placed her arms across her chest and glared.

In a low snarling voice, she said, "I don't know who you are because I've met most of my father's friends and neighbors." Nanette cocked her eyebrow and stared at Lisa.

"How do you know my father? Or did you know my mother? Better yet, what is the real reason for your visit?"

Lisa tried to answer the questions, but Nanette was controlling the tempo of the conversation.

"As you know my father buried my mother a few weeks ago and he's not interested in whatever it is you're trying to peddle."

Lisa's hand flew to her open mouth. She grabbed her chest and sounded indignant. "Well, I never...I thought I would bring your father a..." Nanette cut Lisa off in mid-sentence.

"You can stop the drama. Let me make myself clear. Do not visit my father again. Do not bother to bring him one of those man-catching casseroles. I guess your research didn't reveal the fact that my father is a retired chef. He has no need for a casserole." Nanette's smile was glaring.

Lisa opened her mouth to answer but again she wasn't given the opportunity to explain. Nanette moved within inches of Lisa's face.

She growled in a low whisper and emphasized. "My father's not interested in your casserole or any other woman's casserole."

Turning, Nanette headed back into the house. She stopped and turned back around. Her eyes narrowed.

Firmly, she added, "You won't know when I'll be visiting my father, so don't think you can sniff around here when I leave. If I have anything to do with it, you and no other woman will be bringing a casserole to my father. Do I make myself clear?"

Nanette sneered at Lisa, showing an entire rack of teeth, exhaling a low grumbling sound. Her message was crystal clear.

Lisa opened her mouth, but said nothing. Her attention had switched from Nanette to the wet trickle easing down between her legs. She prayed it was perspiration.

Finally, Lisa mustered up enough courage to nod her head. Backing away from the woman, Lisa turned quickly, walked to her car, got in, and sped off.

CHAPTER 16

Most women would have envied Lisa. Five attractive men were courting her. At first she enjoyed the attention. But as time passed on, she discovered that dating so many men at one time was stressful and tiresome.

Lisa was ecstatic about dating but her preference was to be in a monogamous relationship. After several months, Lisa realized there was only one man she was interested in and that was Patrick Baylor. To focus her energy and attention on him, she decided to stop dating the other men.

After seeing Patrick at least three times a week and every weekend, she was assured of her decision. He was everything she wanted in a man. He was a gentleman, kind, thoughtful, and intelligent. In addition, he showed his admiration for her healthy figure by constantly showering her with compliments.

They had not seen each other in several weeks. Lisa's sister was in the hospital so she had to fly to Maryland. While she was visiting her sister, Patrick was on a cruise. He didn't share with Lisa any details of his trip, but she suspected he was traveling with a female companion.

###

Lisa put finishing touches on her lipstick and checked her makeup before turning off the bathroom light. She had missed Patrick and couldn't wait to see him. She heard the doorbell ring and went to answer it.

"Hi, Patrick. Come in." Lisa thought he looked more handsome than ever. The whiff of his clean manly scent caused her stomach to flutter.

"Hi, beautiful. He kissed her lightly on the lips. Patrick remarked as he walked inside. "You look extremely sexy tonight."

Lisa blushed and thanked him. He pulled a dozen of long stem roses from behind his back, which he had been hiding.

"These are for you."

"They're breathtaking."

She kissed him to show her appreciation. He didn't ease his embrace as he kissed her again.

He pulled away. "We better stop that or we're going to be late for our dinner reservations."

"I agree, but before we leave I better put these roses in a vase."

Patrick didn't want to release her, but he did. They had not made love but he was anticipating the day when they did. He was not going to pressure her into doing something she was not ready to do. He knew how difficult it was going to be for her.

Dinner was wonderful and they shared information about their trips. Patrick did not mention whom he went on the cruise with and Lisa didn't ask.

When they arrived back to her house, Lisa asked Patrick in for an after dinner drink.

"What would you like to drink?"

"A glass of wine." After Lisa fixed two glasses of wine, she joined him. She handed him the glass.

"Why so serious, Patrick?"

"I'm just thinking about us."

"What about us?"

"I was wondering if you were dating anyone else?"

Lisa was curious. "Why?"

"You're not making this easy for me." He raked his fingers through his full head of hair.

"I enjoy your company and I would like to get to know you better, but I can't do that if you're dating other men." He paused for a minute as he tried to read her expression.

"What I'm trying to say and I'm not saying it very well is that I would like for us to date each other exclusively. I mean if that's what you want?"

"Yes, I want that too." He took her in his arms and they kissed.

Over the next several months, Lisa and Patrick were inseparable. They discovered that their personalities were quite different. Lisa enjoyed being around people, but Patrick was a homebody. Their interests made up the differences. They both liked to do indoor, as well as outdoor activities. What pleased Lisa the most was the time they shared gardening, watching birds, and admiring the sunset.

Lisa's life was finally in balance and she couldn't have been happier.

CHAPTER 17

As Kellie punched the numbers in on the alarm system pad, the phone started to ring. For a minute she started to let it ring but thought, *it might be important.*

"Mrs. Olson, I'm calling on behalf of the Director at Regal Care. The Director wants to schedule a meeting with you."

"May I ask what the meeting is about?"

"I wasn't privy to that information. Is 9:30 tomorrow morning convenient for you?"

"Yes and thank you."

When Kellie entered Regal Care, she spoke to the man who was watching the fish in the oversized wall aquarium. At the large picture window was a woman. She was gazing at the pond with the beautiful landscaped waterfall.

Kellie was impressed with Regal Care's décor. It reminded her of sunny Florida with the yellow painted walls, accented with yellow, blue, and white bordered wallpaper. A variety of yellow, brown, and black textured pillows were scattered on the sofas, chairs, and benches. Oriental rugs were placed strategically over the titled floor. The assisted living home had a comfortable, welcoming atmosphere unlike some nursing homes where the air had a stale, disinfected, hospital smell and the appearance to match.

When Kellie approached the reception area, she spoke to Emma, the nurse-in-charge. Then she spoke to Roger's primary nurse, Marcie, but only after she greeted her first. In Kellie's opinion, Emma was one of the nicer nurses.

As Kellie walked down the corridor, she was sure they were talking about her. On several occasions, Kellie had overhead some of the staff discussing the fact that she had married an older man for his money.

Kellie reached the director's office and was shown in by the secretary.

"Good morning, Mrs. Olson, please have a seat."

"I hope everything's okay with my husband."

"Well, that's the reason for the meeting." Kellie watched the worried lines form on the director's forehead.

"Your husband has been with us for about four months. I don't like to make quick judgments about our new residents but your husband isn't adjusting well." The director shifted in her chair.

"Well, this is a major change for him. He needs time to adjust." Kellie heard her voice rise.

The director lowered her voice. "Mrs. Olson, here at Regal Care, we take pride in understanding our newly placed residents. It's more than adjusting, Mr. Olson has been demonstrating signs of aggression."

Kellie was shocked. This was the first time she had been told anything about Roger's potential for violence. The staff had made a mistake.

"What exactly has he done?"

"Well, yesterday, he shoved one of the nurses."

Kellie breathed a sigh of relief. "My husband is paralyzed on his left side and his right side is limited in what he can do. Therefore, it's difficult for me to believe he has enough strength to shove anyone."

"Mrs. Olson, the staff has no reason to lie. You need to understand that our experience tells us that shoving usually leads to hitting. Before Mr. Olson becomes more aggressive, I may have to ask you to find another home for him."

Kellie couldn't believe what she was hearing. "What would she do? Where would she find another place for him?

"Mrs. Olson, are you okay?"

"No, I'm not okay." Kellie was angry. "Please, let me talk to him. I don't want to find another home."

"I understand but I have to think about the staff, as well as the residents. Regal Care recognizes how difficult it is for a person to lose their home and to be placed in a group setting. We are familiar with how new residents may demonstrate their frustration and anger. Regal Care understands that and it's not uncommon but considering the time he's been here, he should be adjusting better."

"I'm sorry and will you apologize to the staff for me. I'll talk to him. I hope we can work this out."

Kellie stood up and exited the office. Instead of visiting Roger, she drove back home.

That evening when Kellie visited Roger, she was careful how she worded her concern.

"Roger, do you like it here?"

Instead of answering Kellie, he shook his head back and forth.

"Roger, stop that."

When he quit shaking his head, he started grunting and making the crude sign language he had learned to use instead of talking. His hand gestures made his message quite clear. He wanted to go home.

"Honey, I wish you could be home with me, but I'm not able to take care of you."

Roger's reply was loudly stated. "L-l-l-let me d-d-d-die."

CHAPTER 18

The dismal, gray cloudy day matched Kellie's bleak outlook on her current situation. The last thing she wanted to do was to go through the agony of searching for a new nursing home.

Before departing Regal Care, she stopped by the Regal Care's ministry office. She knocked on the door, waited for a reply and entered the tiny, windowless office.

"Hi, my name is Kellie Olson. Are you the minister in charge?"

"Yes, so to speak." The man smiled and shook Kellie's hand. "My name is Justin Williams."

"My husband is Roger Olson and he's a resident here. He's in Room 314."

"How can I help you?"

Kellie choked up as she tried to respond. She drew in a breath and exhaled. She didn't want to break down and cry.

"I understand the difficulty my husband is having since being placed in Regal Care. He would rather be home and have me take care of him and I share in his sentiments." Kellie heard her voice crack and grow defensive as she continued to explain.

"Please understand, I had no choice. Before I decided to place my husband at Regal Care, we visited together. He seemed receptive to the idea of assistant living...but..." Her voice faded as she used a tissue to wipe the falling tears.

"Now, I might have to find another nursing home."

Up until that point, Justin had been listening, interjecting nothing. "May I ask why?"

"According to the staff, my husband has been showing signs of aggression."

"I see." Justin made a tent of his hands and leaned forward. "What can I do to help?"

"Could you please talk to him? Since you're a stranger and a minister, you might be able to tell him something…encourage him or…" Kellie halted as sobs replaced her words. She blew her nose.

"The last thing he said was that he wanted to die."

Justin could hear the concern in her voice. "Is this the first time he's voiced such a desire?"

"Yes. I was totally surprised when he said that."

"I wouldn't worry too much. It's not that unusual for a person to express a desire to die, especially with so many changes in a short period of time. I'll visit him and see what I can do."

Justin was Regal Care's volunteer minister. He worked on Tuesdays and Thursdays.

When Mrs. Olson realized that Justin had not visited her husband, she began calling him two or three times a day. Although he tried to explain why he had not had the opportunity to visit her husband, his explanations were unacceptable. As a result, he ended up visiting Mr. Olson on one of his off days.

Justin approached Mr. Olson's closed door, knocked and entered. He crossed the room and stood at the foot of the bed. Mr. Olson must have sensed Justin's presence because his eyes flew open in surprise.

"I'm sorry. I didn't mean to startle you. Good morning. My name is Justin Williams."

Roger cocked his head to the side and stared inquisitively at Justin.

"I'm Regal Care's volunteer minister. Usually I try to visit the new residents when they are first admitted. However, with me working twice a week, this is the first opportunity I've had to visit you."

Although Justin was speaking the truth he was uncomfortable not telling Mr. Olson the real reason for his visit. Justin had not had time to prepare for this visit and he shouldn't have allowed Mrs. Olson to pressure him.

"D-D-D...L-l-let m-m-me d-d-d-die!" Roger shook his head.

"Mr. Olson, change is difficult. I can't begin to understand what you might be going through but if I can help you—" Mr. Olson's voice cut Justin's words off.

"D-D-D...L-l-let m-m-me d-d-d-die!"

In a soothing tone, Justin said, "Mr. Olson, we never know the day or the hour when we might leave this earthly place. The best advice I can offer you is to repent your sins and accept Jesus as your savior. Are you willing to do that?"

Roger nodded his head.

"Let me pray for you. Heavenly Father, we love and praise you. We thank you, Father God, for the gift of salvation that allows us to know that are sins our forgiven because your son died for us. Lord, I pray that you protect Roger and keep him from all evil. Bless Roger, keep him strong, and heal his body. In your precious son's name, I ask these things. Amen."

As Justin finished praying, he noticed Roger struggling but managed to shout. "D-D-D...L-l-let m-m-me d-d-d-die!"

Justin patted his hand and left.

When Justin entered Roger's room, he had failed to close the door completely. Someone was standing in the shadows, outside the slightly ajar door.

CHAPTER 19

Before Kellie reached her destination, she turned her car onto a side street and parked away from the other parked cars. From inside her tote bag, she pulled out a blond wig and put it on, followed by a large white brim hat, and a pair of sunglasses. She peeped in the mirror, from a distance, she was relatively sure no one would be able to describe her facial features. She pulled away from the curb and continued driving.

###

As Kellie sat on the bench, she tugged at the hat brim. She was using extreme caution to keep her face covered.

The sky was blue and free of clouds. The early morning weather forecast for central Florida was supposed to be hot and humid. At the moment, she thought the temperature was pleasant. A slight cool breeze was coming off the water as she sat under a large oak tree. She watched the various boats as her mind drifted to the prearranged directions.

Kellie had received two telephone calls. She played back the conversations. The first call had unnerved her. She wasn't certain if that was her contact person or not. In fact, she thought the voice sounded computerized or it was a tape-recorded message. It was eerie.

"Hello, may I speak to Mrs. Olson?"

"Yes, I'm Mrs. Olson." Before Kellie could respond, the caller continued.

"You need to send the agreed upon money to Let-go Corporation, P.O. Box 3475, Oxford, Florida 34484."

Before Kellie could ask any questions, the phone went dead. After she sent the money, she received the second call.

"Hello, Mrs. Olson." Like the first call, the voice was the same and no time was wasted in giving her instructions.

"Your package will be delivered. On Thursday, you need to go to Lake Harris. Sit on the bench nearest to the wooden pier. Bring a newspaper and place it next to you. Fold the newspaper over once and your package will be delivered."

Again, the phone went dead before Kellie could ask any questions.

When she thought about it, the telephone calls reminded her of television programs or movies involving kidnappings. Similar to the television program or movie, she had been instructed to go to a specific location and wait for further instructions.

In this case, she was sitting in the designated area and waiting as she had been instructed. On TV or in the movie, the police were usually nearby to make an arrest. However, she did not anticipate an appearance from the police, nor would there be any arrests.

Pulling on the brim, she peeped around. Three other people were on the pier. Off to her right, two people were fishing. Across from her was another park bench. A man was sitting with an open book on his lap. The man was too far off for her to see whether or not he was actually reading. From the way his head was bent, he appeared as though he might have been dozing.

Lost in her thoughts, she had not noticed the police officer approaching her. By the time she was aware of him, her heart was pounding rapidly. Her heartbeat was loud enough for anyone nearby to hear it. She warned herself to remain calm as a large drop of sweat trickled down the back of her neck.

Casually, he walked by her and tipped his hat. In return, she lowered her head, to keep her face covered.

"Hello, officer." Her heartbeat did not return to its normal rate until the officer exited the park.

Kellie exhaled and her hands were shaking. Her nerves were frayed and she was eager to leave. According to her watch, she had been waiting for at least twenty minutes.

She thought, *Surely, the package should have been delivered.*

Slowly, she turned her head and glanced over her shoulder. She had not seen anyone walking up behind her, nor had she heard the rustling of the newspaper. With that thought in mind, she unfolded the newspaper.

Kellie tried to contain herself. The package was there and she could leave. Slightly turning around, she made sure no one was standing near her.

Carefully, she picked up the newspaper. As she stood up, her wobbly legs didn't seem as though they would function. Nervousness filled her entire body and she was trembling.

Inwardly, she took a deep breath and blew out. Finally, she was able to walk. Her instinct was to run as fast as she could but she strolled to her parked car.

CHAPTER 20

The night wasn't that unusual, except that a full moon was illuminating the sky. At Regal Care, Emma, the nurse-in-charge was voicing her displeasure to nurse Marcie.

"I hate full moons. I'm not superstitious but I swear bizarre things happen when there's a full moon."

"Come on, Emma. I think its just a coincidence and people seem to associate the events with a full moon."

Emma agreed. "Maybe you're right. But of all the evenings to work, a full moon had to rear its ugly head."

###

All the residents were settled in for the night as the nurses walked softly along the hallways, checking on them and in some cases, waking them for their meds. So far, there had been nothing unusual to report. The evening shift was moving along quickly and Emma was relieved.

When Emma was making rounds, she had a nagging, uncomfortable feeling. She couldn't shake the sensation that someone had been watching her. That was one reason why she hated the rule that residents could have over night guests. Sometimes, when the guests could not sleep, they roamed the halls all hours of the night.

The shift was over and Emma thought, *Thank God.*

They had made it through the night without incident. Emma was making last minute notes on a chart when she heard footsteps, moving rapidly. She glanced up to see Marcie sprinting down the corridor.

When Marcie reached the nurse's station, she was out of breath. She was in full motion as she picked up the phone and started dialing.

Emma watched with curiosity and whispered, "What's wrong?"

Before Marcie could answer, she had to respond to the person she had called. "Yes, this is Marcie Larson. I want to report a death. Mr. Leonard in Room 317." She paused.

"No. I haven't touched the body except to check his pulse even though the monitor is flat lined." She nodded her head. "Okay. Yes, I understand." She hung up the phone.

"What's going on?" Emma questioned as she moved closer to Marcie.

"Didn't you hear me? Mr. Leonard is dead." She pulled in her lower lip and her voice was full of concern.

"This is the sixth death in two weeks. Something isn't right."

"Yeah, like a full moon."

"Seriously Emma. Something's terribly wrong."

"Why do you say that?"

"Come on, Emma. You don't think it's a little unusual that we've had six deaths in such a short span of time?"

"I guess I've been working in nursing homes too long. Let's face it. Most of the people here are in the fourth quarter of their lives. Some of them have illness and some don't. But at any moment, any one of them could be called home to meet their maker."

CHAPTER 21

Although Lisa was not asleep, she was propped up on a pillow in her bed. Her routine in the morning was to read her Bible and pray before getting up. The ringing phone interrupted her.

"Hello."

"Hi, Lisa. Kellie and Arlene are coming over for breakfast this morning. Why don't you join us?" asked Diane.

"Give me a minute and I'll check." Lisa went to the kitchen and surveyed the wall calendar.

"I'm free until six o'clock tonight."

"Great. We'll see you when you get here in a few minutes."

###

When Lisa arrived at Diane's house, Kellie and Arlene were already there. Something was amiss but she wasn't quite sure what it was.

"Good morning, ladies."

In unison, they responded. "Good morning, Lisa."

Diane told them that an egg casserole was in the oven. While it baked, they talked about the construction-taking place, the hurricanes, and what movie they wanted to see later on in the week. Then out of the blue, Diane directed the conversation toward another subject.

"Lisa, are you dating anyone of interest?"

"Uh...well, yes. I'm dating a man named Patrick Baylor."

Diane said, "I thought you were dating someone else?"

"I was dating several men, but I made the decision to date only Patrick. Can I ask why the interest?"

Arlene blurted out. "We're curious as to what happened to the other men you were dating?"

"Yeah, inquiring minds want to know," said Kellie.

"You want to know what?"

"What happened to them?" asked Arlene with impatience lacing her voice.

"How should I know?" Lisa shrugged. "I guess they're dating other women."

Arlene was growing weary of Lisa's answers. "Look, we want to know how you found the men you were dating?"

Defensively, Diane piped up. "Lisa, I told them I might be your friend but you haven't shared anything with me about your love life." She stopped giving Lisa an opportunity to respond.

Lisa thought about their question and she was concerned about how she might respond. But she also knew they would not let her rest in peace if she didn't tell them.

Finally Lisa answered, "The usual places—dating service, newspapers, and the Internet."

Kellie eyed Lisa suspiciously. "That's the truth?"

Through gritted teeth, Lisa said, "Why wouldn't it be?"

"Because we've tried those sources and we had almost no luck," retorted Kellie.

Lisa decided to redirect the focus of the conversation. She had no other choice.

She lowered her voice. "Kellie, it's none of my business, but you're not dating are you?" Lisa paused for a moment not knowing how to continue.

"I'm not one to judge, but what about Roger..." Before Lisa could finish the sentence Arlene cut her off.

"Come on, Lisa, you didn't have to go there. It's nobody's business if Kellie's dating or not."

Swallowing deeply, Kellie stated, "Lisa, you know Roger's in a nursing home and he had a stroke. I know I'm still married but I decided I'm not going to put my life on hold any longer. Life is too short." She chewed on her quivering, lower lip.

"Sometimes I feel like a person who has been given a life sentence in prison. So, yes I'm dating. When I date, I'm discreet and as Arlene stated, it's no one's business but mine. I'm the only one who has to answer to a higher power."

Without warning, Arlene shouted in a louder than usual voice, "How did you find the men? We want to know how you found the men you were dating and the man you're dating now?"

Arlene continued, "It seems to me you don't want to tell us. But since you've dated so many there's no reason not to tell us how you found them." Diane and Kellie joined in and supported Arlene.

CHAPTER 22

The women were all talking at once. Lisa raised her hand to quiet them. Her head was throbbing and her stomach was queasy. She swallowed hard.

"Okay, but I hope you don't think I'm weird. The men I've dated came from the daily newspaper obituaries." The women were wide-eyed as their mouths hung agape.

Suspiciously, Diane asked, "Lisa, how does that work?"

"After I read the obituaries, I attend the funeral service and the repast, and weeks later I take the grieving widower a homemade casserole."

"And that works?" asked Kellie with raised eyebrows.

Lisa spread her hands to her sides. "You've seen the results."

The women wasted no time in wanting to try Lisa's method for identifying, potential men to date. The next morning they gathered at her house. Lisa agreed to provide them with detailed instructions as to how the process worked.

"The first thing we are going to do is to read the obituaries from all the surrounding area newspapers."

Lisa passed out The Daily Sun, Orlando Sentential, The Daily Commercial, and The Star Banner. Lisa kept The Reporter.

Each of the women was instructed to read the obituaries. To Diane, Arlene, and Kellie's surprise, they identified at least four women who died and left behind husbands.

"Now ladies, we have to determine where all the funeral services will be held. Once we do that I'll lay out the ground rules."

"Why do we need rules?" asked Arlene. Her voice was laced with annoyance. Pouting, she said, "I thought this was going to be fun?"

"Well, it can be fun, but it's necessary to have order in doing this. For example, we should not arrive at the services together. Everyone must attend the repast and at no time should we acknowledge that we know one another."

Lisa looked at each woman to see if she understood and if there were any questions. Hearing nothing, she continued with the instructions.

"We must drive ourselves to the funeral service. We must arrive on time. Everyone will attend the repast because that's when you begin to learn information about the widower. Do not volunteer any information about yourselves. Please do not ask questions of any kind. You must become skilled at eavesdropping and be a good listener. Any questions?"

"Lisa, how do we determine if a man will potentially be considered worth dating?" asked Kellie.

"By making mental notes about the man's interests, traits, and lifestyle. And of course, use your instinct."

Whining, Arlene said, "This sounds too complicated."

"It's not that difficult. After we attend the first service, you'll understand the process better."

After writing down the date, time for each service, and the directions, the women were ready. The first service was in several days which gave each of them ample time to prepare.

CHAPTER 23

When the double glass doors opened, Emma gazed up as Mrs. Olson entered. Emma looked at her admiringly.

"You can set your watch by her. Every morning and evening, you know when she is going to arrive."

"Yeah, except when she makes those surprise visits. It's as though she wants to catch someone doing something wrong."

"I don't think that's it. She loves her husband and she wants to make sure he's being taken care of. I would do the same thing except I don't know if I could spend as much time watching a loved one suffer."

"Please, Emma. You're a saint. You would be just like her, except you would be more humble." Marcie continued. "She's so bossy. She orders the staff around as if they were her personal maids and butlers."

"Shhh, she'll hear you. Besides, who do you think is responsible for our paychecks? It's our job to make sure the patients—I mean residents—are given the best care."

"Good morning, Mrs. Olson."

Kellie smiled and thought, *It certainly is a good morning.*

Emma was curious. *I wonder why she's in such a good mood?*

###

When Kellie opened the door to Roger's room, she stood for a moment smiling at him. She walked over to the bed. Gently, she shook him.

"Good morning, Roger dear." Slowly, he opened his eyes.

"How are you feeling this morning?"

Although Roger didn't vocalize his response, he never neglected to react by moving his eyes in the direction of Kellie's voice. At times, his watchful and expressive eyes unnerved her.

Lisa retrieved her Bible from her tote bag and placed it on the floor. She sat in the chair and thumbed through the Bible until she reached Psalms.

"I'm going to read from your favorite book." It was one of her beloved books too because the messages were full of hope.

"I'm reading from Psalm 33:16, 18-20.

"No king is saved by his great army. No warrior escapes by his great strength...

But the Lord looks after those who fear him, those who put their hope in his love.

He saves them from death. And spares their lives in times of hunger. So our hope is in the Lord. He is our help, our shield to protect us."

"Did you enjoy the verses I selected today? Perhaps the verses brought you some comfort. How are your visits with Reverend Williams?"

Roger did not answer but she thought she detected a slight smile when she mentioned his name. She was grateful for Reverend Williams. Since his visits, Roger had been nicer to the staff and there had been no further incidents of him attempting to be violent with anyone.

"When I return this evening, we'll begin a new book by one of your preferred authors, Stuart Woods. Okay?"

He nodded. Although Kellie no longer expected a verbal response from Roger, she chatted to him almost the entire time while visiting him. It was more out of habit than anything.

She laid the Bible down on the nearby table. She closed her eyes and took a deep breath. She stood up and crossed the room.

CHAPTER 24

Nagging pangs of concern, as well as guilt entered Kellie's thoughts. *Was she about to help or harm Roger?*

For a moment, she had an inkling of doubt. But the thought faded and she locked the door.

She turned around and walked back to the tray that was near Roger's bed. She reached into the pocket of her slacks and removed a small bottle. She held the container up and squinted at it. To the naked eye, the liquid would have appeared to be nothing but water.

Roger was observing her. She turned slightly, glancing over her shoulder at him. She couldn't escape his watchful eyes.

Kellie stopped and picked up the spoon that was on the food tray. She approached Roger's bed.

Her hands were shaking. *Be calm,* she whispered.

A stream of perspiration cascaded down the sides of her face and her underarms were damp. Exhaling, she blew out a deep breath of air. She needed to remain composed. As she moved closer to the bed, Roger's eyes began darting back and forth.

Carefully, she poured the liquid onto the spoon, trying not to spill a drop.

Her voice was shaky as she tried to speak with confidence.

"Roger, I have something that will make you feel better." She choked up and a tear fell down her cheek.

Since Roger's hand was under the bedcovers, Kellie leaned firmly into Roger's right side, making sure he could not move his arm. Then, she repositioned herself.

Roger eyed her with suspicion. As Kellie eased the spoon in his mouth, he used his tongue and forced the spoon out.

She lowered the spoon for a moment. In a low, stern whisper, she said, "Roger, don't do that! This is to help you get better."

Kellie wondered how Roger was able to resist with such strength. She raised the spoon again and put it into his mouth. This time she used her strength and shoved the spoon all the way in.

Roger blew against the spoon. He caused some of the liquid to spill out of his mouth. Inwardly, he smiled.

"Darn it!" Quickly, she grabbed a tissue and dabbed at the wet spots on his pajamas and her blouse.

Giving Roger the liquid had been more difficult than Kellie had anticipated. According to the instructions, he had to drink some water. Roger was holding his mouth so taut that she could see the outline of his jaw line. *How was she going to get him to drink?*

Rather than force Roger to drink the water and possibly spill some of it on him, she retrieved a wet washcloth. Cautiously, she squeezed water out of the cloth as she ran it along his mouth.

Kellie stepped away from the bed and blew out a loud sigh. She cautioned herself to stay focused. She rinsed off the spoon and placed it back on the food tray.

Before unlocking the door, she scanned the room. Everything seemed to be in place. She picked up the Bible from the nearby table, crossed the room and unlocked the door.

As she read a passage from the Bible, Roger fell asleep. She watched him. He looked peaceful.

"Well Roger, it's time for me to go." Kissing him, she whispered, "Sweet dreams."

###

Later that afternoon, Justin visited Mr. Olson. He seemed agitated. In addition, Mr. Olson kept repeating the same thing over and over again.

"D-D-D-, l-l-let m-m-m-me d-d-d-die."

"I know but only God knows when that time will be."

Mr. Olson began shaking his head violently. Gently, Justin put his hands on his shoulders in an effort to stop him.

"Please Mr. Olson, you're going to hurt yourself."

Justin raked his hand over his face. He wished he knew how to help Mr. Olson. As Justin was about to leave, Mr. Olson grabbed his arm tightly.

"D-D-D-, l-l-let m-m-m-me d-d-d-die."

Justin listened carefully and asked, "Are you saying, don't let you die?"

He nodded his head and released Justin's arm.

Justin patted his hand and smiled. Justin was happy to hear that Mr. Olson wanted to live, rather than die.

CHAPTER 25

The women gathered at Lisa's house before they prepared to leave for the first funeral service. She wanted to discuss the details one more time to make sure everyone understood exactly what they were doing.

"Are there any questions?"

Arlene wanted to ask some questions but she didn't. Although Lisa went over everything, it now sounded even more complicated. As she started to voice her concerns, she heard Lisa give a warning.

"Ladies, don't be late."

While saying their good-byes, Kellie said, "Ladies, who knows, we might get lucky. We have four services to attend and four men potentially ready to replace his deceased wife."

When Lisa heard Kellie make that statement she cringed.

###

Nervously, Arlene glanced at the clock on the car's dashboard. She had about twenty minutes before the funeral service would begin. She was lost and she couldn't find the directions to the church. She bit hard on her lower lip to keep from crying as she pulled the car onto the shoulder of the road.

Out loud, she said, *Think, Arlene.*

What was she going to do? She couldn't find the directions and she was running out of time. The last thing Lisa said was not to be late.

She needed to remain calm. *Do not panic, no negative thoughts.*

Wiping the perspiration off her forehead, she thought, *The last thing I need now is a hot flash.*

Carefully, she took everything out of her purse, inspecting every piece of paper. The directions weren't there. Then she spotted the newspaper obituary clipping.

Thank God.

Quickly, she used her cell phone to call the funeral home. Waiting for someone to answer, she put everything back in her purse. Finally, she heard a voice. She smiled to herself as she drove, breaking the 35 miles per hour speed limit, all the while praying she wouldn't get a speeding ticket.

When she arrived, she took a few minutes to compose herself. She glanced in the mirror and touched up her makeup. Getting out the car, she straightened her dress and walked in calmly.

She was the last one to arrive as she spotted Lisa, Kellie, and Diane. As discussed, the women had sat in different pew rows and at different vantage points in order to see the widower, relatives, and friends.

Glancing around the chapel, Arlene couldn't believe it. It was over flowing with people. Closely looking from the back to the front, she marched to the front, something she didn't want to do but she didn't have a choice. No sooner did she sit down as a man approached the podium.

"Thank you for coming. I know Clarice would be happy to see so many of her friends and neighbors here today."

The man speaking was James Morrison. He was average height, slender built with a small pouch of a stomach at the waistline. It was hard to determine his age. The majority of his hair was brown with gray highlighting at the front portion of his hairline. His dark brown eyes sparkled and his face was ageless. According to the dates in the program, he had to be at least seventy-four years old.

When he spoke, his voice had a deep, smooth baritone sound. Instead of people comforting him, his voice was soft and soothing.

"Clarice and I were married for forty years. She was the sunshine of my life and my moonlight at night. She was my shining star."

Pausing for a moment, he dabbed at the corner of his eyes. He proceeded by telling funny, personal stories about their courtship, engagement, and marriage. As he talked, it was obvious that James was at peace with this wife's death.

"I'll miss my beloved Clarice, but I'm asking everyone to celebrate her life and not grieve it.

James was an unusual man, Lisa thought. He had set the tone for the service and everyone who spoke after him used the same format. At least ten people told some sort of amusing story about Clarice, especially how she recycled everything.

One woman said Clarice was the only person she knew who could use a paper towel at least ten times before she deemed it ready for the trash. And then, she still questioned whether she could have used it a few more times.

Glancing around the chapel, Lisa could not help but notice there was more smiles than tears. According to the people who spoke, she was a loving, caring individual who had a contagious smile.

Lisa wondered if Arlene, Diane, and Kellie had made the same conclusion as she had about Mr. Morrison?

CHAPTER 26

The repast was held at the Morrison house. The house was crowded with people, including the lanai, and the sunroom. As the women mingled from one group of people to another, they heard nothing but loving comments about Clarice and James.

They had been the *darling* couple, but not without them facing some tragedy. Clarice was in her late thirties before she conceived and gave birth to triples. When their sons were sophomores in college, they were on their way home for spring break.

James and Clarice wanted them to fly home but the boys insisted on driving. From what they were told, a drunk driver hit them head on. They were killed instantly.

In whispered tones, everyone was sharing the same sad story. It seems as though she was never the same after their sons' deaths. At the boys' funeral, she suffered a heart attack. The following year, she had a stroke and to complicate her medical condition, she had high blood pressure, Glaucoma, and depression.

Clarice needed constant care and James refused to place her in a nursing home. Many of their friends feared his health would start to deteriorate in his attempt to care for his wife.

###

The women continued on with their agenda by attending the next three funeral services and repasts. The last three funerals were almost identical to the first service. The only difference was that the last repast was held at the church. Before the repast ended, Lisa carefully told each woman to meet her in the ladies' restroom.

Lisa was the first one to enter with Arlene following behind her.

Excitedly, Arlene gushed, "This is like having a clandestine meeting for a secret society."

Lisa rolled her eyes and put her finger to her lips to quiet Arlene. Kellie walked in and shortly after that, Diane entered.

To no one in particular, Lisa whispered, "Check the stalls to make sure we're alone."

Diane inspected each stall. Then she opened each door to make sure no one was in them.

Finished, Diane stated, "No one's here but us."

Arlene said, "Whew. I don't know about you all, but my feet hurt and I'm hungry." She looked weary. The funeral services had been more fatiguing than she had expected. Although no one else agreed with her, she suspected that they were just as exhausted.

"What are we doing now?" asked Arlene, somewhat irritated. Yawning she said, "I'm tired and I would like to go home and rest."

Lisa was sympathetic to what Arlene was saying. She would give anything to go home, kick off her shoes, change her clothes, and take a long relaxing bath but she had to keep the women focused.

Lisa responded, "I'm sorry that you're worn out, but it's imperative we go over our notes before we forget what we have learned."

Pausing she looked at Arlene to see if she had anything to say. Hearing nothing she continued.

"Please meet me at my house."

CHAPTER 27

Lisa ordered two large pizzas before the women arrived. Although they had attended four repasts, they ate sparingly.

After everyone had their drinks and a slice of pizza they were ready to discuss the events of the day. The food had energized the women as they began talking loudly. Excitedly, they were asking questions regarding the next step in the process.

Instead of answering their question, Lisa directed a question to Arlene. "What happened to you? Why were you so late?"

Nervously, Arlene replied. "I sort of got turned around." Titling her chin upwardly, she proudly said, "But I arrived on time."

Lisa decided not to pursue Arlene's lateness any further. After all, she was there before the service started.

"Well, what do you think?" Lisa asked and smiled waiting for one of them to respond.

Diane gave her impression of the day. "It was tiring and more work than I anticipated. At the first funeral, I was really nervous, concerned, and a little embarrassed. I was so-o-o afraid someone was going to find out that I was a fraud…you know…"

Before she could finish her thought, Lisa asked, "Why were you embarrassed?"

"In a way, what we're doing is somewhat dishonest, you know…not really knowing the deceased or her husband. But I have to say by the second funeral I began to focus on finding out information."

Kellie expressed her thoughts. "I'm in hog heaven. I think we were successful today in identifying four men we all might want to pursue. However, I think we might have a slight problem. How do we decide who gets to take a casserole to which man?" Kellie rushed on to make her intentions known.

"For example, I want to take my casserole to Christopher Franklin."

"Fine, you can have him," said Diane. Arlene didn't respond.

Lisa wanted to hear from each of them. "I think the day was a success and I know you're excited, but let's hear from Arlene.

"It was okay but I'm tired."

"But Arlene, what did you think?" asked Lisa.

"It was okay. At times, it was confusing trying to keep all the dead women straight." Lisa suppressed a laugh.

She moved on. "Let's talk about the men and…"

Before Lisa could continue, the women started talking all at once. Each of them was vocal about the men they had identified as potential dating material. Kellie was firm and would not relent as to the man she wanted.

Arlene suggested, "Let's put the names in a hat and everyone pull a name. It would be a blind draw and fair. There would be no fighting over who gets which man."

Diane said, "I don't care how you do it, but I agree with Arlene, the process should be fair."

Lisa listened as she was reminded of her sisters and how they used to bicker as teenagers over who would be permitted to drive the family car on the weekends. What the women failed to understand was that this was only the first try. If for some reason they didn't like any of the men, they could continue until they found *Mr. Right.*

"Ladies, ladies, ladies. Let's have some order. Before any decisions are made about the men why don't we discuss each man, then choose who gets to take their casserole to which man."

Smiling, Lisa added, "Who knows, Kellie, after you hear about the other men, you might change your mind."

Kellie shook her head and said, "I doubt it. I have a feeling that when I meet Mr. Franklin, we are going to make a connection."

Impatiently, Arlene said, "Can we get started? It's late and I would really like to go home and rest."

CHAPTER 28

The discussion was heated but finally, the women agreed as to who would take which man a casserole. The women were thrilled about their choices and couldn't wait to meet the men. Lisa had to bring the women back to reality.

"Ladies, before you get too excited there is still one last important event that has to be done before you can think about meeting these men."

Arlene interrupted. "Now what do we have to do?" Arlene said sulking and throwing up her hands. "This is way too complicated."

"Arlene, listen while I explain. To seal the deal, you have to make a casserole. That's your entrance ticket into the widower's house. In addition, it's imperative that the casserole you make is extremely delicious, mouth watering, and worth remembering."

"Is this really necessary?" asked Kellie.

"Yes it is. The casserole is the *hook*. Let's face it, most men love to eat. If he enjoys your casserole, he will want to see you again in hope that your other culinary skills are equally good."

Lisa gave instructions for the final step. "Prepare your favorite recipe and bring it to my house. It will be a taste-testing brunch. In addition, please bring a copy of the recipe to share."

###

When the women arrived with their casseroles, the table had been set with Lisa's fine china. Everyone took a seat.

"Before I forget, the feedback I provide is not to hurt anyone's feelings. But if we are to accomplish our goal we must have the finest, appealing, savory casserole."

Lisa explained how the casseroles would be judged. "We're reviewing the recipes to determine quality, ease for making, and cost."

Arlene wanted everyone to taste her recipe first. She had made a Chicken/Broccoli Casserole. She handed each woman a copy of her recipe. They reviewed it without asking any questions.

Chicken/Broccoli Casserole

2 to 3 large chicken breasts, cooked and deboned
½ c mayonnaise
1 Tbsp lemon juice
2 pkg. Frozen broccoli
½ tsp curry powder
2 cans of cream of chicken soup
½ lb Cheddar cheese

Mix soup, mayonnaise, lemon juice and curry powder together. Layer broccoli, chicken (broken into pieces) and soup mixture. Top with grated cheese. Bake at 350 degrees for 40 minutes.

"Arlene, your recipe is straightforward and fairly inexpensive. Now, let's taste it."

Lisa smelled it before tasting it. She chewed slowly. Anxiously, Arlene, Kellie, and Diane waited.

Smiling, Lisa commented. "Arlene, you did a good job. The aroma is enticing. The chicken is moist and the broccoli is crisp. The cheese adds the right amount of flavor. Who wants to go next?"

Diane volunteered. "I'll go."

The same procedure was used. Diane had made one of her favorite casseroles. She passed a copy to everyone.

Lisa studied the recipe closely. "Diane, with the chicken breast, dressing, and all the soup, is this expensive to make?"

"I've never paid attention to the cost."

Arlene commented on the casserole's smell. "It reminds me of Thanksgiving. It must be the dressing."

Chicken Casserole

1 large Pepperidge Farm cornbread or herb dressing
5 or 6 chicken breasts
1 can chicken or mushroom soup
1 cup chicken broth
1 can cream of celery soup
½ stick margarine, melted
1 cup milk

Combine dressing, chicken broth and margarine and set aside. Cook the chicken breasts; remove from bone and cut into small pieces. Mix chicken with the soups and milk. Put ½ of dressing mix in 9 x 13-in baking dish. Pour chicken mixture over dressing. Sprinkle remaining dressing over chicken and bake at 350 degrees for 1 hour.

Kellie spoke first. "Diane, this is really good. If a person didn't want all the Thanksgiving flare, this recipe could be used instead of baking a turkey."

"I agree," said Lisa. "The casserole is scrumptious. In addition, the directions seem easy to follow. The flavor is zesty."

It was Kellie's turn. Hesitantly, she handed Lisa her recipe. Before Lisa read the directions, she said, "Kellie, we can taste your recipe but according to the ingredients, there's no meat. If you make a casserole, meat is a must, unless the man's vegetarian. You know the old saying, most men like meat and potatoes."

"I guess you're right but my specialty is desserts."

"That may be, but why would a man want to try your dessert if your casserole is bland, watery, and not pleasant to the nose?

"At least try my apple pie?"

"I will, but not until we resolve the issue about your casserole recipe. The object is for the man to want more. Your casserole will have the poor man throwing it in the garbage disposal and..." Lisa didn't finish her sentence. Her critique should have been kinder.

Kellie snapped as tears glistened her eyelashes. "I admit my casserole isn't the most inviting but I don't need you to berate me."

"I'm sorry. Why don't you make either Arlene or Diane's recipe?"

"I don't know. Even if I follow the recipe, I'm not sure it will turn out right."

"Okay. "I'll make a casserole for you."

Kellie was right about her pie. The crust was light and fluffy and it wasn't too sweet. The cinnamon and spices were just the right combination. Her pie would certainly be a wonderful finish after eating a mouth-watering casserole.

"I would definitely take your pie along with the casserole," said Diane.

"Will you make me a pie?" asked Arlene.

"Sure. I'll make everyone a pie."

The women were ready to deliver the casseroles, but Lisa told them they had to wait several weeks. The women wanted to make their visits before the time frame established by Lisa, but she had insisted.

"You could visit the men sooner, but I believe you need to wait a respectable time period before showing up on the widower's doorstep. You don't want to appear anxious and possibly raise suspicion."

Lisa paused for a moment as Nanette Adams came to mind and added. "In addition, if the man has children, they will probably be gone by that time."

When the day arrived, the women were more nervous than they had expected. Arlene was the only one to voice her concern.

"I've been looking forward to today, but now that the day is here, I don't think I can go through with it."

Lisa encouraged, "Sure you can."

Immediately, the other women chimed in. They stated they were nervous too, but they were treating the delivery as if they were taking the casserole to a grieving friend.

CHAPTER 29

Arlene was raising and waving her hand like a child in elementary school, waiting for the teacher to call on her. Arlene was anxious to discuss her experience. Finally Lisa acknowledged her.

"Go ahead, Arlene. Tell us about your delivery."

"As you know, my casserole was delivered to James Morrison. He is really a nice man. He was gracious and happy that I brought him the casserole. He invited me to eat it with him and I did."

Arlene took a sip of her ice tea. She began again. "He likes to talk. He told me everything about his move to The Villages, the death of his wife, and his interests."

Proudly, she said, I was a good listener. I couldn't believe how he showered me with compliments about my dress, hair, and overall appearance."

She smiled, sat back and relaxed and as an after thought, she added, "Oh yeah and I have a dinner date with him for next week."

"That's it!" Kellie rolled her eyes.

"The way you were acting, I thought you had something juicy to tell us." Lisa and Diane glared at Kellie.

Before words were said that everyone would regret, Lisa said gently, "Kellie, that was exciting for Arlene especially since she was hesitant about delivery the casserole to James. Why don't you go next?"

"Well my intuition did not fail me. Christopher Franklin is everything I expected and more. He's intelligent, handsome, but has a bad boy edge to his looks, and financially secure."

Suspiciously, Arlene asked, "How did you figure that out?"

"He lives in one of the premier homes on the Nancy Lopez Golf Course, on the third tee."

"If Chris has a major flaw, I would say it's that he's been married three times. Two of the marriages ended in divorce and we know what happened to wife number three."

Kellie paused, trying to think if she had forgotten anything. Then she added with a twinkle in her eye. "I accepted his invitation to dinner, next week."

Satisfied with her recap, she folded her hands in her lap. Since she said nothing else, Lisa turned to Diane.

"I'm not quite as excited as you two. The man I delivered the casserole to may be out of my league. Did any of you realize how young the widower was?" No one responded and shook their heads in the negative.

"We screwed up somewhere in our research. I remember going to the funeral and the repast but somehow I didn't focus on his boyish looks." Diane paused and looked at Arlene.

"Aren't you the one who identified Sam Childers?"

Arlene responded with attitude. "I don't remember. Why? What's the problem?"

"Because he's in his late thirties."

"Are you sure?" Arlene asked with an expression of disbelief.

"Duh! I'm sure. Remember I took him the casserole." Diane was annoyed.

"Well, what is he doing in The Villages?" asked Arlene. She seemed confused.

Diane explained, "His wife was older than him."

"Oh, he likes older women?" smirked Arlene.

"I'd be careful. He might like older women because he likes 'Sugar Mommas.'" You know like a 'Sugar Daddy'?" Arlene sniggered and continued.

"Maybe you should rethink whether you want to date someone that much younger than you. Besides you need a man, who wants to waste time training a boy?" Arlene giggled.

Indignantly, Diane responded. "Listen, I'm not fifty yet so why not date him?"

"In some ways, you might be better off with a younger man," groaned Kellie.

Softly, Diane said, "Well, despite what I'm saying I accepted his invitation to dinner."

The women were victorious. Lisa was impressed and happy about their successes. It usually took her several casserole deliveries before she was asked out on a date.

They were in high spirits and extremely pleased with their discoveries and could not wait for their first dates. They reminded Lisa of teenaged girls, giggling, joking, and discussing what they were going to wear on their first dates.

CHAPTER 30

Extremely satisfied with the dating results, Diane, Arlene, and Kellie were delighted with an idea they had. They could not wait to share it with Lisa. Kellie was the spokesperson.

"Lisa, we've talked it over and we want to start a dating service, using your system."

"What? Are you crazy?"

"Why are you so surprised at our suggestion?"

"I guess...uh..."

The last thing Lisa wanted to do was to enter into a business venture of this type. She sat trying to find the right words to explain her hesitancy about their suggestion.

"Lisa I don't think you have a choice but to join us," Kellie said with confidence.

"I disagree. I'm supportive of you all. If you want to start a dating service, I wish you nothing but success. But I don't want to be a part of the business enterprise."

"Why, may I ask?" Arlene stood with her hands on her hips, staring at Lisa through narrowed eyes.

Lisa did not respond immediately. She wanted to select her words carefully. It was important for the women to understand her reasoning.

"This seems innocent enough, but I think what I did and what I shared with you all will only lead to more dishonesty and lies. I'm not comfortable with the trickery and deceit."

Kellie shook her head and let out a snort. "Oh, suddenly you have scruples."

Lisa wanted to counter what Kellie had said, but she didn't want to debate the issue and its merits. Lisa attempted a different defense.

"How can I go into a business that is somehow morally wrong?"

The deafening silence that filled the room told Lisa that she had hit a nerve. No longer wanting to discuss this matter, Lisa stood up as if dismissing the subject. As she made steps toward the door to leave, Kellie stepped in front of her. She crossed her arms and stared fiercely at Lisa.

Lisa's voice was firm. "Kellie, please understand. I don't want to be a part of this dating scheme. However, if you all want to start it, I have no problem with you doing it."

Lisa made a move forward but Kellie remained firm and said, "We're not finished with this conversation."

"As far as I'm concerned, I'm done. And of course, your secret is safe with me."

Kellie chuckled. "I know you won't tell our secret just like we won't tell your secret."

Lisa looked at Kellie's piercing eyes. Kellie's eyebrow was raised and a wicked smile crossed her lips.

"How did Patrick like your casserole?"

Lisa fell quiet. She didn't have to answer Kellie's question and she knew it.

"Are you blackmailing me?"

"I wouldn't call it blackmail."

"Then what do you call it?"

"A friendly persuasive technique that will help you make the right decision about our business proposition."

CHAPTER 31

Despite Lisa's resistance, the business was formed. They scheduled their first meeting.

The first item for discussion was the selection of the business name. The women debated on a number of names, such as Over-Aged Dating Service, Women Only Dating Service. Everyone agreed that the names weren't elegant or catchy. While the discussion continued, Diane kept returning to one name.

"Listen ladies, The Casserole Delivery Service represents a part of how we will be selecting the men."

Hearing Diane's explanation, the women agreed on the name. The women discussed and at times even argued about who would be eligible to use the service; how would they advertise; and how many matches would be made for each woman?"

After much debate, decisions were finally made. The service would be for women only. Even though Diane wasn't fifty, they agreed that the service would only match women who were fifty and older. They would not advertise. The business would operate out of Diane's house since she had a three-bedroom villa home with an office.

All clientele had to be referred by a woman who had previously used the service. A private investigator would be hired to conduct rigorous background checks on each man and woman. The investigation was to ensure that the men and women were single, heterosexual, and financially secure. Diane, Arlene, Kellie, and Lisa would make every effort to protect the confidentiality of each client, especially the men.

After several months, Lisa was surprised as to how efficiently the business was operating. Each woman had her own strengths and weaknesses that complimented each other. The women were constantly perfecting Lisa's original process.

Diane developed and maintained a database for the men and women matched. In addition, the women were working solo that enabled them to attend more services and repasts.

The only difficulty the dating service encountered was Arlene's forgetfulness. It had not become a major issue, but occasionally, she forgot which funeral service she was supposed to attend. This resulted in Arlene going to the same service as one of the other women.

To combat the problem, the women began printing out the address and the directions for her. On the day of the scheduled service, Kellie would check with Arlene to review where she was supposed to go.

At one of the meetings, Arlene expressed her concern about the reminders.

"If I can't be trusted then maybe I shouldn't be a business partner."

Lisa tried to reassure her. "Don't be silly, Arlene. We all have moments when we have a hard time remembering our name. So please don't be offended about the reminders."

"No one else seems to be receiving reminders regarding their funeral service assignments."

To avoid upsetting Arlene any more than she was, Lisa said, "From time to time, I call Kellie and ask her about my assignment. The difference is that I never say anything about it."

CHAPTER 32

The business was more lucrative than the women had expected. Many of their clients were not only satisfied with their matches, but also thrilled with the results.

The database did not track the success of the matches. However, the feedback the women received indicated that about 90 percent of the men and women matched had ended in engagements, marriages, or co-habitation.

Rosa Michaels had been the first paying client of The Casserole Delivery Service and had been the most consistent when referring clients. Rosa had been the primary reason why the business was thriving.

Once a month the women could depend on Rosa to provide them with ten or more referrals. Generally, Rosa met with them on the third Thursday of the month. To everyone's surprise they received a request from Rosa for a meeting.

When Rosa arrived, she didn't waste their time. "Ladies, your service has been incredible and I truly appreciate what you have done for me. As a result, I'm not sure how to start."

The women looked at each other with concern. Since it was Rosa's meeting, they did not rush her as she sat chewing her lower lip.

"I have no way of knowing but I think I might refer more women to your service than any of your other clients."

The women did not confirm what Rosa said. They remained quiet as she continued.

"Next week I was prepared to provide you with twelve referrals but I've been having second thoughts."

The women's eyes widened as they exchanged expressions of surprise. Arlene let out a gasp.

"Why? Have we done something wrong?"

"This is not personal. I want to assure you that you have done nothing wrong. I mean I refer so many women but what benefits do I receive?" No one answered her.

Rosa smiled. "I've devised three options for your consideration. One, you could make me a partner; two, you could give me a referral fee; or three, I could start my own business." Rosa paused and thought she would let the women mull over what she had said.

Carefully, Lisa responded. "Rosa, I think I speak for everyone when I say you've taken us by surprise. We need time to discuss your options."

"I would like an answer before I refer another woman." Rosa chuckled. "Besides, I know how you find the men for your service and I don't think you would like women to know who they're dating."

Kellie had a slight edge to her voice. "I'm curious, Rosa, how do we find our men?"

"Keep in mind I'm not bothered by your method. After all, there is no way I would have found James Winters on my own."

Again Kellie insisted. "I asked, how do we find our men?"

"You recruit them like escort services. You visit cities, run an ad, interview the men and make matches, accordingly. That's why you do an investigation background check."

Lisa had the worse poker face. To hide her facial expression, she lowered her head and didn't dare look at Diane, Arlene, or Kellie. She would not have been able to keep from laughing.

An uncomfortable silence hovered over the room. It was a noticeable length of time before anyone spoke.

Arlene spoke up. Her voice was calm as she turned to Rosa. "We really appreciate you wanting to be one of our partners. But as you know, we haven't been in business that long. At this time, we aren't ready for any type of expansion. However, the minute we decide to increase our business, you will be the first person to be considered."

The women smiled and nodded their heads. Each of them was thankful for Arlene's quick wit and response.

"I see. Is there anything I can do to change your mind?"

All the women shook their heads. They thought Rosa was finished but she continued.

"I'm sure you all won't mind a little competition then?"

Diane responded firmly. "We truly value your candor Rosa and we understand if you don't want to refer any more women to us."

Rosa was taken back at what Diane had said. To cover up her reaction, she changed the subject.

"As you know I constantly thank you for my match. I will always be obliged." She glanced at the women and with a wide smile and excitement she gushed, "James and I are getting married."

"What?" Kellie's eyes were wide as she added, "What wonderful news!"

"Congratulations. When is the wedding?" asked Arlene.

"We haven't set the date but when we do, you'll be the first to know." Then with emphasis, she added. "After all, it was through your service that I was able to find a man."

The Rosa's pasted smile faded as her face took on a wickedness that caused the hair on the back of Lisa's neck to stand on edge.

CHAPTER 33

Diane was eight years older than Sam. The age difference would not have been that bothersome but Sam's boyish features made him appear much younger than he was.

Sometimes when they were on a date Diane was actually embarrassed by the stares and remarks from people they encountered. Intellectually, she knew age was only a number but being constantly reminded of it was a challenge.

In addition, Diane decided not to tell her son and daughter about dating a younger man. She would tell them once she was sure where their relationship was headed. She believed her children would be supportive of her dating but worried how they would react to her dating a younger man?

How could any woman resist Sam? He was a gorgeous, sensitive man. Any woman would have loved dating him. With his handsome young face and muscular toned body, she often questioned why he was dating her?

At first Diane thought she was merely filling a void in Sam's life. But the more time they spent together, she realized they connected on a level that was beyond sex.

When Diane delivered the casserole to Sam he had been living in The Villages. From what Sam shared with Diane he moved because the house was filled with too many painful memories of his life with his late wife.

Diane had no problem finding his apartment. It was a new complex located in Leesburg.

Diane stepped off the elevator and inspected the apartment numbers. Odd numbers were on the right and even on the left. Apartment number 210 was down the hall on the left.

Sam had planned to move to North Carolina the day after his wife's funeral service. But he had a contract with his job and they would not release him from it.

At first he was angry that he had been unable to move but if he had relocated he would have never met Diane. The last thing he wanted in his life was a woman but Diane was like a fresh breath of air. Their relationship started out as friends but it turned into something more.

His friends and relatives warned him about getting involved with a woman so soon after his wife's death. They believed he was trying to fill a void as well as replace his wife, Wendie. His sister was the most vocal about his dating.

He attempted to explain to everyone that he was not trying to replace Wendie. Diane and Wendie were so dissimilar. Their outer appearance was nothing alike and their personalities were different as the sun and the moon. The only commonality was that both women were older than him.

Diane brought him pleasure. He could not understand why no one saw how happy he was and it was partially because of Diane. No one wanted to hear him talk about his newly found romance, so he quit talking about her.

Sam cooked one of the three chicken dishes he knew how to make. The recipe was one of his mother's favorite recipes. He put chicken pieces in a baking pan and covered the pieces with wild rice and mushroom soup. To go along with the chicken dish, he fixed a salad. For dessert, he had bought an apple pie from Perkins Restaurant.

The fresh flowers and lit candles added ambiance. Sam smiled as he took one last glance around the room before answering the doorbell.

CHAPTER 34

Diane was wearing a blue dress with a plunging neckline. When Sam opened the door, he stood dreamy eyed and fixated on her slightly exposed breasts. His face reddened as unsavory thoughts drifted through his head.

At that moment, Sam asked his deceased wife to forgive him. He would always love her but he was falling in love with Diane.

Standing in the doorway, Diane wondered what was wrong with Sam. He had the most bizarre facial expression as he looked at her.

"Hi Sam. Is everything okay?"

"No...I mean...yes."

Grabbing her hand, he led her into the apartment. He kissed her so deeply and with so much feeling that Diane's heart was pounding rapidly. It left her lightheaded and woozy.

Diane pulled away from the embrace and gazed into his eyes. "We better stop before we lose our appetite." Diane's face reddened and quickly she changed the subject.

"What's that delectable smell?" Diane asked about the food but what really filled her nostrils and made her hungry was the whiff of Sam's cologne.

"My mother's secret chicken dish. Anyone could make the recipe but I promised her that I would never reveal the family secret."

Dinner was delicious. Diane could not remember a time in her life when she felt alive and loved, even being married to her ex-husband for twenty years.

After they cleared the table, put the dishes in the dishwasher, and put the leftovers in the refrigerator, Sam could resist no longer. He gathered Diane into his arms. As he gazed into her eyes, his breathing was hot and uneven.

Easing his embrace, Sam said, "Diane, I know we haven't been dating that long and I recently lost a wife but I'm falling in love with you."

Pausing, he looked at her. He wanted to see if he could read her reaction to what he had said.

Her legs were wobbly. Sam's words left her too weak to speak. She never expected to hear those words from him. When she first met Sam, she decided to date him as a new experience and for fun. In addition, she referred to him as her "boy toy" and had used him accordingly.

But now he was saying he was falling in love with her. How did she react to that? As she was about to reveal her feelings, her eyes were drawn to a photograph sitting on a nearby table. She wanted to inspect the framed picture more closely.

"Diane…Diane. Did I shock you that much?" A nervous laugh escaped Sam.

"Uh…no. I'm sorry." Diane was confused and needed some air.

"Let me say it again. I think I'm falling in love with you." He waited.

Diane eased out of his embrace and sat on the sofa. "Sam, please sit down."

He could not believe it. He had shared his feelings with Diane and she was rejecting him. How could he have been wrong about her?

"Sam, you're a wonderful man but I think it's too soon for you to know what you're feeling…" Her voice trailed off.

He raked his hand over his face, frustrated. He wished people would stop telling him how he felt. He knew what was in his heart.

He was not a teenager experiencing his first crush or rebounding from a bad breakup, divorce, or death.

"Diane, please listen to me. I know what I feel. I thought you felt the same way."

"Sam, I enjoy being with you but is it love? I'm not sure."

Before Diane could say anything else, Sam gathered her in his arms. He kissed her with such feeling that Diane went numb. Without protest from her, he laid her back on the sofa. He kissed her. This time it was longer and deeper. Diane's body was on edge with her skin prickling from his touch.

Besides her ex-husband she had never made love to another man. However, it was Sam who caused Diane to experience the true meaning of sensuality, sexuality, and passion. Regardless of Sam's age, he was the teacher and Diane was the student during their lovemaking.

After each lovemaking session, Diane swore she would never let it to happen again. But here she was again allowing her body to be swept into ecstasy.

Sam's long sensual kisses and his intimate touching caused her body to respond to his seductive rhythmic moves. His seductive male aroma and the heat of his body were over powering. No longer in control, she gave freely to being pleasured.

As the enthralling sensuality flowed between them and they were about to reach a level of rapture, Diane panicked. Her breathing was heavy and her mind was in a weakened state as she murmured, "Sam, you need…"

CHAPTER 35

When Kellie delivered Christopher Franklin a casserole, there was an instant connection as well as an attraction. Everyone called him Chris. His father was Christopher.

At first, the conversations between Kellie and Chris were strained. Kellie thought it was because he was still grieving his wife. The more time they spent together, she realized that he was complex, as well as egotistical.

Despite the magnetic attraction between them, Kellie disliked his lack of communication skills. When they had a conversation, she always pictured a tugboat pulling a barge, sluggish and deliberate. In addition, Chris was slow to share personal information.

One evening, he confided, "I've been married three times. Two of the women, I divorced. In the case of both women, we weren't compatible and had little in common. Since I don't believe in wasting my time trying to fix things that are beyond repair, I ended the marriages."

Kellie never knew how to respond to some of his cold, emotionless statements. It wasn't until Chris talked about his third wife, Sara, that Kellie detected a different side of him.

"Sara and I were married for five years. She was beautiful as well as intelligent. We had been on a cruise. As we made port in Miami, she had a major heart attack. She died on her way to the hospital. She didn't suffer. I was glad she didn't linger on because I know I could not have given up my life to care for her."

Kellie's ears perked up when she heard what he said about not being able to care for a sick wife. Hearing him, it made her think that perhaps Chris would understand her situation with Roger?

She wasn't that different from Chris. If she was truthful, she knew she didn't want Roger to suffer. He would be better off...she didn't finish her thought. She should have been guilt ridden but she wasn't. For the first time in years, she was beginning to live. She compared herself to a rat. She was cornered and all she was trying to do was survive.

Oh well. She needed to put those thoughts out of her head and concentrate on getting ready for her date. She and Chris were driving to Orlando for a dinner theater performance.

When Chris arrived, Kellie could not believe he had rented a limousine. It was the longest limo she had ever seen.

When she greeted him, he bowed and said, "Your carriage awaits you, my lady."

Inside the limo, she couldn't believe how spacious it was. It had all kinds of amenities—television, radio, phone, and a bar filled with an array of drinks.

On the drive to dinner, Chris closed the private tinted window that separated the driver from the passengers.

Chris kissed Kellie deeply and ran his hand under her dress, up her thigh and between her legs. Firmly, Kellie put her hand on his, indicating she wanted him to stop.

Chris whispered in her ear. "Have you ever made love in a limousine?" He then entered his tongue in her ear. It tantalized her into making a low, deep groaning sound.

Breathing heavily, she answered. "No."

"Then relax. I'll show you what you've been missing."

He ran his hand inside her dress and grasped her breast. She flew her head back. "Chris…" She moaned. "I don't think this is a good idea."

Chris ignored her protests and continued to seduce her with his kisses and intimate touching.

"What about the driver?"

Whispering with a breathy voice, Chris said, "He can't see or hear what we're doing."

He kissed her long and hard. As much as Kellie wanted him to stop, her body betrayed her. She melted into his grinding hip movements as if they were one. When their lovemaking ended, Kellie was flush as her body tingled with satisfaction.

However, she was conflicted with emotional turmoil. How could she allow herself to be tempted into acting so scandalous in public? At that moment she could not explain her mixed emotions of anger, embarrassment, delight, and pleasure.

Inwardly, she smiled and thought. *You're never too old to start experiencing new sexual adventures.*

CHAPTER 36

When Kellie arrived at Regal Care, she was walking with renewed energy and it showed. Smiling, she blushed as she recalled the limo ride. She wanted to share her experience with Lisa, Diane, and Arlene but she wondered what they would think of her?

"Good morning, Emma."

"Good morning, Mrs. Olson."

Kellie's greeting was delivered with a cheerfulness she couldn't hide. She was in high spirits and she didn't care who detected it.

Emma watched Mrs. Olson as she strolled down the corridor. Emma thought her appearance was glowing. In addition, Emma heard Mrs. Olson humming a show tune.

When Kellie opened Roger's room door, she stared at him for a minute. His eyes were closed. When she touched his arm, his eyes popped open wide.

Kellie jumped as her hand flew to her chest. Hysteria set in for a moment. As she inhaled and exhaled, she composed herself.

Calmly, she spoke, "Good morning, Roger."

As quickly as he had opened his eyes, he closed them. Kellie thought his movements were sluggish. He didn't seem alert. Gently, she shook him. Gradually, he opened his eyes.

"Roger, your coloring appears better but you seem as though you don't feel well?"

No response, but he kept his eyes open as she continued to rattle on about the weather and bits and pieces of news that she had read in the morning newspaper. When she reached into her tote bag and brought forth the clear liquid, Roger watched her intently.

Kellie whispered in his ear, "Before the day gets too hectic around here, I have something for you. Please don't fight me. This is as beneficial for you as it is for me."

The temptation was to increase the dosage she had been giving Roger but she decided she better follow the instructions.

Each time she gave Roger a spoonful, he fought her. Despite his efforts, she had managed to give him the recommended doses. According to the instructions, if given in proper amounts, no evidence of the substance could be detected during an autopsy.

"I know you didn't want it, but it's good for you. You'll see."

Closely, Kellie watched Roger. His facial expression had a glow of content and peacefulness.

"Roger, I want the best for you. I hope you know that. I would never do anything to harm you."

Kellie closed her eyes and said a quick prayer. *Lord, I'm putting Roger in your hands. I hope you will not let him suffer too much longer.*

"Well dear, I can't stay this morning. I have a doctor's appointment but I'll be back this evening."

He closed his eyes. Kellie didn't know if he was responding to her explanation or if he was tired. She shook him softly, but he did not open his eyes. His breathing was slow and even.

"Roger I'll see you later. You rest."

Kellie kissed him lightly on the lips. She stood back and watched him for a minute.

"I love you, Roger. May you rest in peace."

###

Weekly, Lisa had been visiting Roger. When she entered his room, he was asleep. She didn't want to wake him. When she finished praying for him, his eyes opened.

"Hi Roger, I thought you were sleeping and I didn't want to wake you. How are you doing today?"

"F-f-f-fine."

"Good. I guess I missed Kellie?"

He nodded his head.

"I'm not going to stay. You seem a little drowsy today."

"D-d-don't let me die."

Lisa patted his hand. "Don't worry. You're not going to die. My grandmother used to say, 'The devil doesn't want you and God's not ready for you.' Besides I can see you improving every day. I'll keep praying for you."

A tear fell down Roger's face. He was frustrated and weary. No one appeared to understand. He knew he was running out of time.

CHAPTER 37

Rather than dine out, Lisa offered to cook dinner for Patrick. She grilled fish, steamed mixed vegetables, made a salad, and peach cobbler was for dessert.

"Darling, you could make any man happy with the meals you cook."

Weakly, Lisa smiled at him. It always made her nervous when he made comments about her cooking. His compliments made her recall when she was delivering casseroles to men.

Dinner was quieter than usual. Lisa sensed that something was wrong. She wasn't going to press the issue. After dinner, Patrick was serious.

Lisa was sitting on the sofa when he started talking. "Lisa, I think you know how I feel about you."

Not responding to him, Lisa sat with her hands folded in her lap. Slowly, she watched him walk toward her. Joining her on the sofa, he sat close to her. He picked up her hands. Looking deeply into her eyes, he leaned in as if he was going to kiss her but changed his mind.

Silence occupied the room as if it was a third party. Patiently Lisa waited. Patrick was having difficulty in telling her whatever was on his mind. Finally, she heard his baritone voice. Slowly and purposely, he started.

"Life is short…what I mean is…with each birthday I grow a little older."

Patrick cleared his throat. He attempted to make eye contact with Lisa but was unable because the words were sticking in his throat. Looking up at him, she wondered why he was having such difficulty talking to her.

She thought how this was not typical of him. He was stumbling and fumbling over his words. His attempts at speaking were similar to someone who had a speech impediment.

Up until this moment, Patrick had always been forthright. Smiling slightly, she recalled when he asked her to take a blood test for sexually transmitted diseases.

Calmly, he had asked her without blinking an eye. She on the other hand had been flabbergasted and embarrassed. He said he wanted to be prepared in case they might want to have sex.

If he could be bold enough to ask her about something that delicate then he should have no problem telling her what was bothering him. The only subject that might make him uncomfortable was if he decided he no longer wanted to date her.

Patrick was one of the more eligible bachelors in the area. Like other retirement communities, there were plenty of single, widowed, and divorced women but a lack of men.

Daily, it was nothing for a woman to invite Patrick to breakfast, lunch, or dinner. He was handsome, healthy, financially secure, generous, and an overall nice, considerate guy. Most of the single women were envious of Lisa for being the one who nabbed him.

Patiently and uncomplaining, Lisa waited. He was biting his lower lip as a look of fright and concern covered his face. Unexpectedly, he blurted out.

"Will you marry me?"

Wide eyed, Lisa was stunned. To mask any other expression, she smiled widely. Under normal circumstances she would have been ecstatic.

Patrick was the first man she met since the death of her husband who had made an imprint on her heart. He made her remember what it was like to be sensual, attractive, and desirable to a man.

Patrick was watching her. She knew he was waiting for a response but she was having difficulty speaking.

CHAPTER 38

Uneasiness, sadness, and concern filled Lisa's body as she tried to formulate a respond to his proposal. As he watched the troubled expression on Lisa's face, he could only wonder what was wrong.

"Are you okay? Maybe I was premature in asking you to marry me so soon in our relationship. I'm sorry..." His voice died into nothingness.

Looking at Patrick, Lisa's smile was rueful. Her voice had taken on a coarseness that caused her to clear her throat.

"Patrick, I'm so flattered and pleasantly surprised. This was the last thing I expected." Pausing for a minute, Lisa was buying time as she searched for her next words.

"Uh...as you said, we haven't known each other that long." Interrupting Lisa, Patrick interjected.

"I know but we aren't promised tomorrow. I don't want to waste any more time trying to figure out our likes, dislikes and interests. After we marry, we can learn what we need to know about each other." This time Lisa interrupted him.

"Patrick, I don't understand the urgency. Yes, we're growing older but we shouldn't take marriage lightly. Both of us had wonderful first marriages and I would hate for our second marriage to end in divorce."

She hurried on. "Besides, what will your children think?"

"I've already told them about us and they are happy for me…us."

With a raised eyebrow, Patrick eyed Lisa. He saw tears sparkling her eyelashes. He wondered if those were happy or sad tears?

As much as he wanted to marry Lisa he didn't want to jeopardize their current relationship. If she needed more time to consider his proposal then he would have to be patient.

In a soothing voice, Lisa tried to explain. "Patrick, I care deeply for you. When I have to make life-altering decisions I have to consider the pros and cons of the situation. I don't think our age should be the motivating factor for rushing into marriage. In addition, you don't know everything about me." Lisa continued before he could rebuke what she was saying.

"I do think we—no I have to speak for myself. You caught me by surprise. I need time to think about this. I'm not saying I don't want to marry you. It's just that… Her voice trailed off as she noticed Patrick's heartbreaking expression.

The last thing Lisa wanted to do was to hurt Patrick and she didn't want to lose him. To regain Patrick's confidence that she was seriously considering his proposal, Lisa quickly added.

"I know you want a yes or no answer but I can't give that to you now. I have some personal and professional business I have to address. I promise that as soon as I straighten everything out I will give you an answer."

"If that's all it will take, then please take all the time you need. I promise to be patient."

Lisa was grateful for Patrick's understanding. Weakly, she smiled as he grabbed her and they kissed.

Patrick was ecstatic but he could not miss Lisa's melancholy eyes and the worried lines across her forehead. He wanted to help her but he decided not to press her about what was really bothering her.

Closing the door behind Patrick, Lisa leaned against it. Tears running down her cheeks, she covered her mouth to smother her loud sobbing.

CHAPTER 39

Lisa did not like the reflection she saw in the bathroom mirror. Off and on throughout the night, her tears had flown freely. The result was red, puffy eyes and regardless of how much make-up she used, it would be impossible to hide the deep, dark circles under them.

She had slept fretfully. Her concerns about the business and dreams about Patrick discovering the truth caused her to have nightmares.

The business should never have been formed, thought Lisa angrily.

She stepped into the shower and turned on the hot water, followed by cold water. After the shower, she carefully applied her makeup. She put on a bright yellow sundress in an attempt to offset her haggard appearance.

This was the morning for their official business meeting. The first order of business would be to discuss their client's dating progress, requests, and matches. The second order of business was for each woman to provide an update on the man they were dating.

The success of the dating service was not only making their clients delighted but the owners were just as satisfied. Kellie and Diane were still dating their original matches. Arlene had chosen to date several men.

Sometimes, the women were still amazed at the results of how they found the men they were dating. Diane and Kellie thought they had found the ultimate, wonderful man.

After discussing the business aspects of the service, the women were ready to share how their relationships were progressing. Although Lisa had met Patrick before the business was formed it was her hope to tell them about his proposal. As usual, Diane reported first.

"Ladies, I know you all are all happy with the man you're dating but I know most women would kill to be dating my man."

"Yeah. Yeah. Yeah," said Arlene sarcastically. Then she snorted. "You remind us all the time."

Kellie said, "Okay, give us the latest details."

"Well, I don't have to remind you of the fact he's my boy toy."

In an annoyed voice, Arlene asked, "How can we forget?"

"It's hard not to remind myself of the fact he's younger than me and so-o-o gorgeous. He's everything you would expect a man to be. When we have a date, it's nice to be able to wear any style heels without having to worry about my height. After all he is over six feet inches tall."

She hated to boast but this was the first time she had experienced dating a man who was good-looking, caring, and wanted her. She hurried along before the women became annoyed with her.

"When we went to the beach, every woman was admiring his chiseled arms and his muscled, shapely legs. He could easily have been a male model." With a sly smile, she grinned. "Or even a male stripper, like those Chippendale dancers."

Every time Diane talked about Sam, the women visibly showed their displeasure as well as concern. It was Lisa who voiced her fears.

"Diane, I know you're having fun dating Sam…but maybe you should consider dating someone closer to your age."

"Come on, he's not that much younger than me."

Lisa tried to be as diplomatic as possible without making Diane angry. "Whatever. What I'm trying to say is that you might want to think about having a more meaningful relationship other than…s-e-x. I don't want to see you hurt."

Diane was defensive and resented what Lisa was implying. She proceeded with self-assurance. "I know you're worried about me and maybe I've been too cavalier referring to him as my *boy toy*. But our relationship is not all sex." She proceeded but her voice lowered.

"I know what I'm doing. I'm not going to fall in love with him. My husband…I stand corrected…ex-husband had an affair with a woman ten years younger than him and married her. Why can't a woman do the same thing?"

"You're right." Arlene defended Diane. "Men date younger women all the time. No one seems to care. But don't let an older woman date a younger man—it's still a no-no, as if the woman was committing a sin. So you go, girl."

Arlene gave Diane thumbs up while Lisa and Kellie laughed as they gave her high-fives.

CHAPTER 40

Arlene was hesitant to talk about the men she had been dating. In comparison to Diane, her experiences sounded boring.

"I don't have much to report since the last time we talked. In fact, after hearing Diane, my dating is down right dull."

Diane urged. "We want to hear about the men you've been dating. It can't be that bad."

"Not really, but…."

Lisa pleaded. "Tell us."

Kellie added. "Don't make us beg."

"Okay." Arlene smiled mischievously. "You all know I'm dating two men."

"I don't remember you dating two men." Diane looked curiously at Lisa and Kellie.

With a smirk on her lips, Kellie said, "And you said, you have nothing exciting to report."

"Well, I'm not sure I'm ready to make a commitment to one man."

"Are you enjoying dating two men?"

"It's rather flattering but sometimes I get them confused. Once I even called them the wrong name."

Diane always asked, "What do they look like?"

"Well, Harold Woodson is about my height, slender, average looks but an overall nice guy. Bill Sanders is about average height, a little stocky, balding with a great personality and a wonderful sense of humor."

"At our age, who cares about looks, as long as they're healthy, breathing, and not drooling." Lisa wanted to keep the conversation light, trying to hide her concern.

"At least we don't have to worry about Arlene acting irresponsible, like me. She's playing it safe with the men she has chosen to date," Diane stated.

Lisa wondered if Diane had not been listening carefully to Arlene. She said the one man she's dating was Harold Woodson—that was her deceased husband.

Despite Lisa's trepidation, she encouraged. "Tell us more about the two men."

Arlene smiled and with confidence as she shared. "The biggest difference between the men is that Bill has no children while Harold has a daughter like me."

"What about your daughter?" asked Kellie.

"My daughter met Bill. I was kind of anxious about introducing her to him, but she was supportive." Arlene was not answering Lisa's question and Diane reminded her.

"That's not what Lisa asked. Maybe, you didn't understand the question. Did your daughter have a preference between the two men?"

Arlene looked at Diane with sympathy. Despite Diane's meanness at times, Arlene was sympathetic. She suspected Diane was in the beginning stages of menopause and her moods and attitudes needed understanding. Arlene recalled her menopausal days. In fact she still experienced hot flashes. Menopause was not easy.

"I'm sorry that I digressed. Surprisingly, my daughter was not much help. She thought..." Arlene stopped.

Her facial expression was perplexed, as she asked no one in particular. "Am I really dating two men? Why would I do that?"

CHAPTER 41

Rather than wait for Arlene to continue, Kellie gushed excitedly. "Chris is so-o-o-o right for me. I think I'm in love." She held her hand over her heart.

"Don't look at me like that," said Kellie as she noticed the disapproving looks.

"I know I should have kept to my standard rule of never dating a man more than twice, but I couldn't help myself."

"Well, does he know about Roger?" asked Arlene.

"Let's put it this way, I haven't told him. I tried several times but I couldn't find the right words."

Lisa rolled her eyes and thought, *I wonder why not?*

Diane wanted to know. "Why did you break your rule?"

"Okay but hold on to your seats. I wasn't going to tell you all but we made love in the backseat of a limo." She smiled and rushed on while blinking her false eyelashes.

"He thinks that I'm the most beautiful woman on earth. Seriously, the most important thing for me at this time is that he's as healthy as Samson. I have fallen so deeply in love with him. Every time I'm with him, it's as if I'm a teenaged school girl going out with the quarterback."

For the next several minutes, Kellie boasted about Chris. She told them she had to be the luckiest woman on earth. Worried lines crossed the faces of Diane, Lisa, and Arlene.

Lisa spoke her mind. "I don't want to burst your bubble, but what about Roger? Remember, the man in the nursing home, your husband."

The happiness that Kellie had displayed disappeared into a hurtful expression. She was disappointed her friends and business partners could not be compassionate. It was during these tense discussions that Kellie was thankful for her support group.

In a low tone Kellie said, "I haven't forgotten about my husband. Nothing has changed. He's still my number one priority."

Kellie sounded like a pouting child who couldn't have her way. "I think I deserve some sort of a life. Who knows, Roger could out live me. Chris, unlike Roger, makes me feel like a woman. I know it's not fair to compare the two men but all I can think about is why can't I be happy?"

Lisa looked at Kellie and wanted to say something supportive, but what could she say? She remained quiet.

Usually Diane was sympathetic toward Kellie's situation. But she was finding difficulty listening to Kellie discuss a man, other than her husband. It made Diane angry as her ex-husband came to mind. He had cheated on her and it hurt. As much as Kellie considered herself "single," she wasn't.

Arlene had intended to keep her mouth shut but her words spilled out. "Kellie, I know you have always said you were single but in reality, you're married." Arlene noticed the tears about to spill from Kellie's eyes but she proceeded.

"In the past, when you dated, you never allowed yourself to be emotionally attached. Unfortunately, your husband happens to be in a nursing home. If you want to date, fine, and I understand that's your business. But at least be honest and tell Chris the truth about your marital status."

Arlene stared at Kellie, but she didn't respond. Perhaps, Arlene had said too much.

Diane whispered, "There is another alternative. You could tell Roger the truth. Then you wouldn't have to have pangs of guilt about dating Chris."

CHAPTER 42

With rehabilitation, Roger was gaining more and more of his strength. Although he had to drag his left leg he was capable of walking with a cane.

He had not demonstrated his newly acquired skills to Kellie. He wanted to surprise her. When she saw how well he was progressing, she would have no reason not to take him home.

Roger's ears perked up as he heard an unusual amount of activity in the corridor. He still wasn't able to get out of the bed on his own. He pushed the button for Marcie. When she appeared, he would find out what was going on.

"Good morning Mr. Olson."

"G-g-good m-m-m-morning."

"Every day your speech is improving. I know you're wife must be excited about your progress."

He smiled and nodded. His wife had no idea.

"You're up early. Do you need to use the bathroom?"

He nodded again.

"Mr. Olson, I told you I want you to use those vocal cords."

"O-o-okay. W-w-what's a-ll t-t-the n-n-noise?"

Marcie leaned close to Mr. Olson and whispered, "The director was told that the police received an anonymous tip about residents being murdered here at Regal Care."

"O-o-h m-m-my." Roger acted surprised but the suspicions he had about wrongdoing had been confirmed.

"To make matters worse, someone, probably the same anonymous person who called the police, tipped off the media. It's like a circus around here. Regal Care is in total chaos."

Roger smiled. Kellie didn't like Marcie, but he loved her. Regal Care wasn't her favorite employer and she didn't mind sharing gossip with him.

"Did I mention that the police arrived with a search warrant?"

"N-n-n-no. W-w-w-what r-r-r t-t-they l-l-look-f-f-f-for?"

She gave him a roguish smile. "Dead bodies."

"W-w-whoa."

"The director is beside herself. She asked that the police allow the staff to awaken the residents to help explain what was taking place, answer questions, and to alleviate some of the fears."

Roger was back in bed. Marcie had bathed and dressed him.

"Mr. Olson I'm going to have to leave you now. Expect the police. It's my understanding that once the residents are up, bathed, dressed, and fed, the police will be searching the facility. In addition, everyone will probably be questioned."

"T-t-thanks."

Although the police came into Roger's room, no one asked him a single question. The director or nurse Emma probably said he couldn't talk.

It took several hours of searching the premises before the police left. According to Marcie, nothing had been found. No dead bodies, no missing residents, and nothing unusual to indicate that any crime had been committed.

Roger would have given anything if the police had to string up the yellow, crime scene tape. Marcie stated that the director had been able to keep the media off the premises but she was worried about how this would be reported in the newspaper and on the local news channels?

CHAPTER 43

Large raindrops were hitting against the acrylic windows of Lisa's lanai. The sound was soothing to her. She opened the morning newspaper.

Lisa liked to scan the paper first then decide which individual articles she would read in detail. Before she turned back to the front page, a headline caught her attention. Carefully, she read it. Her eyes grew wide.

She glanced at the clock mounted on the wall. It was probably too early to call Kellie but she did anyway.

The phone rang three times. The answering machine began at the same time Lisa heard Kellie's voice.

Her voice was breathy. "Hello. Hello."

"Kellie, this is Lisa. Hi. I'm sorry I'm calling so early but have you had a chance to read the morning newspaper?"

"No...I just stepped out the shower. Why?"

"Well..." Firmly, Lisa instructed. "Go get your paper!"

"Lisa..."

Lisa cut her off. With urgency in her voice, she pleaded. "Please, Kellie! It's important!"

"Okay. Let me go to the kitchen where I left it. Hold on." Kellie was annoyed as she thought. *Lisa could be such a drama queen at times.*

"Lisa, I have the paper."

"Good. Turn to page three and go about half way down to a column on the left hand side."

Kellie did as she was told. She didn't know exactly what she was looking for as she scanned the articles. Suddenly, she stopped. Her hand flew to her mouth and she sat down in the nearby chair.

Kellie should have read the article by now, thought Lisa. "Kellie. Kellie. Are you still there?"

Weakly, she said, "Yes, I'm here. It's just that the article. I'm more than surprised. If this is true, Regal Care certainly has been able to keep this quiet for some time."

"That's what I was thinking. And no one has notified you about this?"

"No-o-o. But I can understand why."

"Roger was okay when you visited him last night?"

"Uh...yes...as far as I know, he's fine...I mean if he wasn't, surely I would have received a call." Kellie paused for a moment.

"Kellie, I know you haven't had a chance to digest all of this but what are you going to do about Roger? I mean are you afraid for him?"

"I don't know if he's in any danger. Besides, I have to find out exactly what's going on before I jump to any conclusions. I'm sure Regal Care is going to be bombarded with calls from anyone who reads this article."

"I'm sure they are. I don't understand it. What is this world coming to?"

"I know, Lisa. Listen, I need to finish dressing and then I'm on my way to Regal Care."

"Of course. I'm sorry I called so early but I thought you would want to know."

"Please, Lisa. I appreciate you calling me. I'll call you later and tell you what I find out."

CHAPTER 44

Before Kellie finished dressing, she headed to the kitchen. She turned on the coffee maker.

Returning to the kitchen, Kellie fixed a cup of coffee. She glanced at the clock. She thought about skipping breakfast and going to Regal Care but it was too early. The director wouldn't be in her office yet. She went back and forth for several minutes debating what she should do.

Finally she decided to fix breakfast. Lisa scrambled an egg and buttered her toast. As she ate, her thoughts drifted to the last conversation she had with Lisa, Diane, and Arlene.

Her friends had disappointed her. She was tired of people judging her. Of all people, she thought they would have understood what her life had been since Roger's stroke. After their meeting, she now knew she was alone regarding her marriage views, caring for an ailing spouse, and dating.

Before she met Chris she had been satisfied with her life. She had friends, went to the movies, dinner—basically she did what she wanted to do. She rarely complained about caring for Roger. Visiting Roger had never been a chore; she did what she would have expected him to do had the tables been reversed.

What had changed? She met Chris. He had complicated her life. Initially, she had intended to treat him like all the other men she had dated. However, Chris had used unusual persuasive techniques that caused her to fall prey to his lovemaking.

When she met Chris, there had been an immediate magnetism between them. Before she knew it, her heart was involved. She had not intended to fall in love with him. In fact, she never thought she would love another except for Roger.

The phone interrupted her thoughts. It was probably Diane or Arlene calling about the newspaper article.

"Hello."

"Hello, Mrs. Olson. This is the Regal Care Nursing Home. Dr. Bernstein would like to speak to you. Please hold."

"Hello, Mrs. Olson."

"Hello."

"Is it possible for you to come to Regal Care, now?"

"What's happened?" Kellie's heart was beating rapidly.

"I would rather not discuss it on the phone."

"Okay. I'll be right there."

Hurriedly, Kellie drove to Regal Care. She wondered if Roger had…no, she wasn't going to jump to conclusions.

Horror settled in her throat and traveled to her stomach. With everything happening at Regal Care, she wondered if? She admonished herself to stop it. She would discover soon enough why she had been summoned to Regal Care.

When Kellie entered the nursing home, she walked quickly to Dr. Bernstein's office. She stood at the secretary's desk and waited patiently while she finished typing.

"Good morning, Mrs. Olson." She buzzed the doctor on the intercom and instructed Kellie to go in.

Taking a deep breath, she went in. The doctor stood up from behind his desk and greeted her when she entered.

"Good morning, Mrs. Olson. Thanks for coming so quickly. Please have a seat."

Kellie sat on the nearby sofa. Dr. Bernstein sat in the chair oppose the sofa. Dr. Bernstein folded his hands as he began to speak.

"Mrs. Olson, have you read the morning newspaper?"

"Yes and I have to say I was quite disturbed."

He ran his fingers through his hair. "I understand. It's upsetting to me as well as the staff." Dr. Bernstein took a deep breath. "However, this has nothing to do with that article." He looked at Kellie.

"Mrs. Olson, during the night, something happened to your husband." Before Dr. Bernstein could continue Kellie started screaming.

"Oh no, poor Roger. Oh God."

Dr. Bernstein tried to calm her. "Mrs. Olson, please. Take some deep breaths."

Kellie did as she was told. Tears were flowing.

"Mrs. Olson, your husband slipped into a coma. We didn't discover it until this morning and I called you immediately."

"What caused him to go into a coma? Oh no…you don't think?"

"Please, Mrs. Olson, don't jump to conclusions. The coma was probably a result of his most recent stroke."

She stared at him and listened. Before she could ask a question or say anything, she heard Dr. Bernstein talking fast.

"The good news is that your husband didn't die. In addition, as he has requested, he has been placed on oxygen, a feeding tube, and other monitoring devices. We'll do everything we can to make him comfortable."

"When will you know if someone was trying to…"

"I'm ninety-nine percent certain that your husband's condition is due to natural causes. With his age and the recent stroke, I don't believe anyone was trying to cause him harm."

Kellie chewed on the inside of her cheek. "Can I see him?"

"Of course. He has been moved from his suite to what we call our hospital wing of the nursing home."

Kellie thanked the doctor and left his office. As she walked down the corridor, her jaws were tight. The words she couldn't shake were, "he's in a coma."

###

Sitting in the parking lot, Kellie made a telephone call. When she heard a voice, she said, "Roger's in a coma."

"Did you follow the instructions?"

"Yes, to the letter. What am I supposed to do?"

"Nothing. You'll have to let nature take its course."

CHAPTER 45

When Kellie arrived home she was mentally and physically drained. She knew she had not escaped Lisa seeing her pull into the driveway.

Rather than talk to Lisa later, Kellie decided to do it now. When she got out of the car, she strolled over to her house.

To Kellie's surprise, Lisa had not been sitting on the lanai. She rang the doorbell. When Lisa answered the door and saw Kellie's distraught expression, she reached out and hugged her.

At that moment, Kellie was unable to control her emotions. She held onto Lisa and sobbed uncontrollably. Lisa led Kellie to a chair and disappeared. When Lisa returned she handed Kellie a glass of water and a box of tissues.

Kellie blew her nose before she took a sip of water. "Thanks, Lisa." Through tears, she said, "I'm sorry."

"You have nothing to be sorry about. That's what friends are for." Although Lisa was anxious to hear about Roger and Regal Care, she waited until Kellie was ready to talk.

"You're probably wondering how Roger's doing?" Kellie looked at Lisa and she nodded.

"After we talked, I received a call from Roger's doctor at Regal Care. But..." She took a deep breath. "When I met with the doctor I wasn't prepared for what the doctor told me." Kellie started sobbing again but managed to say, "Roger's in a coma."

Lisa gasped. "Oh, you poor dear. I'm so sorry. When did this happen?"

"Last night or either this morning. They're not sure."

Lisa pondered for a moment before inquiring. "I hope Roger's recent health problems aren't due to the alleged murders that we read about in the newspaper?"

"No. The doctor assured me that Roger's current condition was a result of his age and the most recent stroke."

"But I wonder if someone tried to kill him but instead he slipped into a coma."

"No. No. I sort of implied that but the doctor said he was ninety-nine percent certain that Roger's condition was due to natural causes."

"How can the doctor be so sure?"

"I don't know but the doctor said that Regal Care is conducting an investigation into all the deaths. So far, there's no evidence to support that any murders have been committed."

"But what about the newspaper article and cases like Roger?"

Kellie's voice became irritated. "Why are you including Roger in that category?" She didn't wait for Lisa to respond.

"Roger isn't dead. He's in a coma. Besides, the doctor said the deaths are probably nothing but a coincidence. The problem came about when the coroner's office questioned the number of autopsies he had recently performed from Regal Care."

Kellie stopped and offered no additional information. They both sat quiet, neither woman making eye contact.

Sadly, Kellie said, "I have to be realistic and not jump to conclusions. As the doctor stated, most of Regal Care's residents are elderly and some quite sick. Therefore, no one should be surprised when a death occurs."

Lisa thought about what Kellie said and agreed. "You're probably right." Carefully Lisa added. "But aren't you concerned that these deaths are being dismissed just because of the resident's age?"

Kellie's response was filled with irritation. "I'm concerned but considering Roger's age and his medical condition, what would be suspicious if he were to die? In Regal Care's defense, I know that Roger has received nothing but excellent care since I placed him there."

CHAPTER 46

Patiently, Diane sat in the doctor's office. She had been in for her yearly check-up, which she hated. However, she was no different than millions of other women. The Pap smear—it was a necessary evil.

She was almost one hundred percent sure she was at the beginning stages of menopause. Despite some of the horrid stories and side affects of hot flashes, night sweats, and mood swings, she was enjoying not having her monthly. She smiled, the one positive benefit of menopause.

"Mrs. Benson, I am so sorry I've kept you waiting but I had a telephone call I had to take."

"I understand. Unexpected things happen in a doctor's office."

"Thanks for being so understanding." The doctor reviewed her chart before she continued.

"From my exam, I think you're doing fine. However, I do want you to come to the office tomorrow for some blood work."

"Why?"

"Well, I might be premature, but I'm almost positive your problems are because you're pregnant." Diane had to hold onto the desk for support.

"What are you talking about?"

"When I examined you, I would say you might be about four weeks."

Diane did not allow the doctor to finish her sentence. She was curious.

"I'm forty-eight years old. How could this happen?"

She chuckled. "You tell me."

"No. I'm serious. I thought I was beyond the age of having children. I mean I'm too old to have a…." Diane paused, unable to say the word.

A thought occurred to her. She was no longer married. Without warning, she started laughing until tears rolled down her face.

"Mrs. Benson, are you okay?"

Diane started to tell the doctor about her situation, but changed her mind. "Yes. I'm fine."

The doctor didn't have to know that she was on a fixed income with limited medical coverage, a divorced woman with grown, married children, and in a relationship with a younger man.

"Then you're set. Once I receive the results of your blood work you can schedule an appointment where we'll discuss prenatal care and other precautions that will be taken during your pregnancy. On your way out, remember to schedule an appointment for your blood work. Then we'll know for sure. Congratulations and have a great afternoon."

When Diane left the doctor's office, she was not convinced she was pregnant. She didn't care what the doctor's exam revealed.

Not realizing it, Diane had driven to Walgreens, a drugstore, and was pulling into a parking space. Inside the store, she walked directly to the aisle where the home pregnancy kits were sold.

She would go home and take the test, as well as have the blood test tomorrow. Then she would have a stiff drink and have a really good laugh. She wasted no time in taking the test.

Patiently, she waited. She must have stared at the kit results for at least fifteen minutes. Her eyes had to be deceiving her.

CHAPTER 47

Despite Diane's personal problems, she had to focus on the business. She called an emergency meeting. She wondered if any of the women had any idea that The Casserole Delivery Service was in trouble.

Arlene was the first to arrive. "Good morning, what smells so good?"

"Coffee cake."

"You're determined to make us all fat."

"Not really, I made it with Splenda. It's a Weight Watchers' recipe."

"Well, that helps."

Standing near the door, Arlene answered it. Kellie and Lisa had arrived.

"Good morning, ladies, come on in."

Both women asked what was the delicious smell. Before Diane could answer, she had taken the coffee cake out the oven and placed it on the rack to cool.

"Everyone, help yourselves and we can begin the meeting." Everyone fixed their drinks, got a piece of coffee cake, and sat down at the table.

The Casserole Delivery meetings were casual. The business had no CEO, but they did have an accountant. Since Diane had the most computer skills, she was in charge of developing and maintaining their database. Most of their meetings began with the minutes read by Kellie who served as the secretary. However, since this was not a scheduled meeting, there were no minutes to be read.

"You're probably wondering why I called this meeting. Yesterday was the first time I had a chance to review our database and I think we might have a slight problem."

"What do you mean?" Kellie could not imagine the business having any type of a problem.

"The database indicates we have more women clients than men to match the requests."

"How did that happen?" asked Lisa.

"How would I know?" Diane answered defensively and then softened her voice. "I guess we've been too successful."

"If you think about it, we haven't been identifying that many men lately. In fact, we only added three new male names to the database in three week. But for some reason, we have six new female clients."

Diane had the women's attention. They stopped eating and focused on what she had said.

Kellie was cynical. "I don't think our problem is that bad."

"Excuse me," responded Lisa. "We can't possibly continue taking on new clients when we can't match the ones already in the system."

No one had a comment. The silence covered the room like a comforter on a bed. It was almost suffocating.

Diane had to support Lisa. "You're right. I don't see how to solve this problem."

Kellie started to say something but she stopped. She had an idea but as she mulled it over, her instinct told her that this was not the time to share it.

Lisa knew what they needed to do and she had to say it. In addition, it would solve another problem—Rosa.

"Maybe this is the time to consider dissolving the business."

"Lisa we are not going to end this business," said Kellie with conviction.

"Do you have any idea how well we have done financially? Aside from the money, every day someone tells me how happy they are with their matched mate," said Diane.

"You're both right about the matches and the money but if we don't have the men to match the requests, then what?" Lisa wanted to know.

Confidently, Kellie said, "I don't know, but we'll figure it out."

Lisa turned to Diane. "How many requests do we have and how many men are available?"

Diane handed them the report she had prepared. They had fifteen requests and only ten potential men. Kellie read the report and didn't see the problem.

Kellie directed her comment to Lisa. "If I'm reading this report correctly, we are only short five men. That's nothing. Five women could die tomorrow, leaving behind a spouse. I think you've over reacted Diane." Before saying anything else, Kellie studied the report more closely.

Diane didn't respond to Kellie. The numbers may seem close but the fact remains that the women leaving behind husbands had slowed.

Arlene asked, "Diane, do you believe we have a problem?"

"Yes I do. If I did not think it was a problem, I wouldn't have brought it up." Kellie made a face and pressed on.

"Diane, if we match all the requests we have now and hold off from taking on new clients temporarily, will that solve our problem?"

"I don't honestly know."

Lisa wondered off on her own concerns for a moment. She wondered if she should bring up Patrick's proposal. Maybe if she told them, they might... Before Lisa could finish her thought, Diane brought her back into the conversation.

"Lisa, at what point do you suggest we dissolve the business?"

"I say, let's end it now."

Arlene wanted to know. "What do we do with the women waiting for a match?"

Lisa explained, "Nothing. We end the business like any other business."

Angrily, Kellie said, "Lisa, you never wanted to be a part of this business. So, ending it is your only solution?"

"You're right," Lisa said so quietly that the women could barely hear her.

Kellie was determined. "I think we need to wait and see what happens. Who knows? We might have a solution and just haven't explored all our options."

Lisa's eyes were pleading as she looked at Diane. She shrugged. Then she directed her eyes at Arlene who lowered her head.

It was three against one.

CHAPTER 48

Lisa needed to hear a friendly voice. She hoped Patrick was home as she dialed his number.

"Hi Patrick. How are you?"

"Fine."

"What's wrong? You sound tired."

Lisa wanted to tell Patrick what was bothering her but she couldn't. Since his proposal, she had not told Diane, Arlene, and Kellie. It was as if every time she had the opportunity, something stopped her from telling them. Since she had not told them, she certainly could not give Patrick an answer to his marriage proposal.

"I'm okay. I think I've been working too many hours."

Patrick had not brought up the subject but when they married, he did not want Lisa to work. He wanted her to sell her portion of the business. He wanted them to travel and do whatever else they wanted and the business could possibly interfere with their plans. He should bring the subject up now but he was afraid. He tried a different approach.

"Have you ever thought about cutting back your hours?"

Lisa did not answer Patrick right away. If he only knew, she did not want to work at all. She wanted so badly to end her partnership with the dating service but there was no way. Kellie was not going to allow her to quit.

"Can we talk about something else? I don't want to talk about the dating service."

Patrick wondered why not? He would try again.

"Lisa, I know you're tired but maybe you should…" Lisa did not let him finish his sentence.

"I told you I was tired." Her voice had a sharp edge to it and she did not hide her annoyance.

"And I told you I had enough business talk for one day."

He didn't have to be hit over the head with a sledgehammer. As directed, he changed the subject but he knew Lisa well enough to know something was bothering her. Maybe with time she would share with him what it was.

"How about dinner?"

"Tonight?"

"Yes, tonight. If you don't want to go I understand."

"No. I want to see you. Where do you want to go?" Lisa's voice had softened.

"What about the Red Lobster in Leesburg?"

"I would prefer some place quiet."

"I know just the right place. Why don't you come over to my house? I'll call for Chinese take out. How does that sound?"

"Patrick." Lisa stopped. Her tears were mounting up. She forgot she had not answered him as she heard his inquiring voice.

"Lisa, are you okay?"

"I'm okay. Your idea sounds what the doctor ordered."

She did not have the words to express how much she appreciated him and his thoughtfulness. She was overwhelmed with emotion with everything going on in her life.

"I'll see you in about one hour."

"Lisa, I love you."

Although Lisa found comfort in hearing those words, it was too much for her as she broke down into sobs. Quickly, she hung up the phone.

CHAPTER 49

Sam was perturbed at Diane. He couldn't understand why she had not called him. She mentioned having a doctor's appointment and she would call but to date, he had not heard from her. The only thing he knew was that she was having her annual check-up.

From Diane's mood swings he suspected she might be in the beginning stages of menopause. He knew how difficult menopause was for a woman. He recalled vividly how difficult it had been for his late wife.

Calling several times a day was not cool, but all kinds of things were going through his head. It was driving him crazy. He really wanted—no needed to talk to Diane.

Since she had not returned his calls, he had not been able to sleep, eat, or work. The last two days, he called into his job, stating he was sick. His job had not questioned him. Since the death of Wendie, his supervisor had been more than generous and understanding when he requested time off.

He had been napping off and on all day. He had no energy. Although he had lied when he called into work about being sick, his stomach was queasy and he had chills earlier. Going to the kitchen, he thought he would fix a bowl of soup and drink a hot cup of tea. Maybe that would settle his stomach. The headache might have been from him not eating all day. As he opened the refrigerator, the phone rang.

"Hello." When he heard Diane's voice, he gasped. His heart skipped a beat and his palms started sweating.

"Hi, Diane, I've missed you so…" He stopped. He didn't want to sound overly anxious.

"Hi, Diane."

"Sam, I need to see you."

"What about tonight?"

She thought before she answered. "Not tonight."

"What about tomorrow?" He hoped he was not pushing too hard, but he wanted a definite commitment from her as to when they would get together.

"Okay, tomorrow."

"Do you want to come over here or go out to dinner?"

"What about me coming over there?"

"What time?"

"Let's say, seven."

Sam was anxious to see and talk to her. He had so many questions. How was she doing? What has she been doing? And what did the doctor say? However, she hung up before he had an opportunity to ask her any of his questions. Her voice sounded strained, as if she had been reading from a paper.

When Diane hung up, she took a deep breath. No mistake had been made. Blood tests do not lie. After taking the blood test, Diane had gotten an independent blood test and the two tests came up with the same results. She was pregnant.

How could she have been so irresponsible? It was as if she was eighteen years old instead of forty-eight years old. She had all the emotions of any woman who discovers she's pregnant—panic, anger, and fear. Not to mention, the fear of how the father of her baby was going to react.

She wanted to tell her friends but she could only wonder what they would say? One thing for sure, she did not want lectures about how irresponsible she had been.

CHAPTER 50

Amanda Roberts was at a turning point in her life and it was time to ask for help. She was at her wits end. Sipping a cup of coffee, she remembered—the woman she met at the hospital. Frantically, she searched for the woman's business card. She found it.

Dialing the number, Amanda focused on the woman's name on the business card.

"Hello, may I please speak to Kellie Olson."

"This is she."

"Hi, Kellie. My name is Amanda Roberts. I don't know if you remember me or not but we met at the hospital."

Amanda waited for Kellie to acknowledge what she was saying but when she heard nothing she continued. "I talked to you in the hospital waiting room."

"Oh yes. I remember now. Your husband had a stroke. How's he doing?"

"That's why I'm calling. Do you have a minute?"

"Sure. What's up?"

"I'm researching nursing facilities and I remember you saying that you were placing your husband in an assistant living home. How is it working for you?"

"I did place my husband in the Regal Care Assistant Living Complex. It was a difficult decision because Roger wanted me to take him home."

"I understand but how is the facility? Are you satisfied with it? How did your husband adjust?"

Kellie exhaled. "To start off, my husband and I had visited the home before I had to make the decision. We both were impressed with Regal Care. It met my requirements. But…my husband has had a difficult time adjusting." Kellie paused for a minute.

"I don't know how to ask this but Regal Care has been in the newspaper lately about irregularities in some of the deaths. How has that affected your opinion about the home?"

Kellie wanted to be honest with Amanda. "I have to say that I've been bothered by the allegations but I spoke to one of the doctors. He isn't sure if the deaths have actually been murders. Apparently the suspicions came about because of the number of autopsies that were performed."

"Is a police investigation being conducted?" asked Amanda.

"Yes there is. Until I'm told differently, I'm confident about Regal Care providing outstanding care for their residents."

"You certainly sound convincing but I don't know. I mean for someone to possibly be killing some of the patients deliberately. I would feel terrible if something happened to my husband after placing him there."

"Listen, I have an idea. Remember the support group I told you about?"

"Yes, why?"

"Tomorrow is our regular meeting. Why don't you join us?"

"I don't know. I'm not sure I want to discuss my concerns with strangers. Besides I have to work."

"The meeting is held at seven o'clock. At least try it one time. I think it might help you. It wasn't until I joined the group that I realized I wasn't alone."

"Okay."

They talked for several more minutes. Kellie provided Amanda with the meeting place, time, and directions.

CHAPTER 51

Timidly, Amanda opened the door to the Oxford Community Center. When she walked in, about twenty women were talking, drinking coffee, and eating cookies. Kellie spotted Amanda.

Breathless with excitement, Kellie greeted her. "I wasn't sure you'd come. I'm happy you decided to come."

"Hi, Kellie."

"Come on in. Let me introduce you to everyone." As Kellie made the last introduction, a woman was calling the meeting to order.

"Ladies, welcome. Do we have any new visitors tonight?"

Amanda was the only new person. She was grateful she wasn't required to tell them anything about her life. In fact, the meeting was casual.

"As you know, we meet weekly. At the meetings, everything is confidential. You are not alone and can share whatever issues you might be wrestling with. We are here to support you. You are not alone."

"Hi, my name is Kellie Olson."

All the women responded, "Hi, Kellie."

Although Amanda had never attended an AA meeting, that's what came to mind as she listened.

"I'm married to a man who is seventeen years older than me. Currently, I placed him in a nursing home. I have accepted my plight in that I cannot change what has happened. I've taken steps to turn my troubles over to a higher power. Because of certain decisions, I need your help. I'm dating a man that I think I'm falling in love with."

Amanda tried not to react but she knew her eyes were wide. Thank God, her mouth did not fall open. She continued to listen as several women stood up, introduced themselves, and discussed issues involving daycare, aging parents, and work.

Once everyone was finished, the meeting leader began the discussion but in general terms. Amanda noticed that she was careful not to give advice or make any judgments. Sometimes, a woman would make a suggestion or offered prayer.

After the questions had been discussed, the leader gave a general briefing on assisted deaths. Once again, Amanda was trying to keep her reactions inward.

"I know that some of you have been discussing this among yourselves and have not brought it formally to the group. Since there seems to be some interest I thought I would bring it forth today."

Until the subject was broached, the women had been talkative and animated. But now, they sat as if their lips were sealed.

Cautiously, Amanda broke the silence. "Let's say that if someone was to assist their spouse in their death, do you recognize that you're committing murder?"

Indignantly, a woman responded. "Sometimes, there's extenuating circumstances."

Amanda didn't want to discuss the morality but murder is murder. She wasn't about to judge and she could sympathize but she had to take a stand even if she was the lone wolf. "Regardless of the reasons, it is murder."

The leader interjected. "I understand both viewpoints but I believe we shouldn't dismiss the reason for the death. We're talking about a loved one who would welcome the end of their suffering. If it's your husband who is pleading with you to end his

143

life because he can no longer endure the pain, what would you do, Amanda?"

"Well…uh…" Amanda was stuttering. She had not considered that reasoning but as a DA, it would still be murder. In addition, a jury would certainly view it as murder.

Amanda was relieved when the meeting ended. It was not what she had expected. She waited for Kellie because she had some questions she did not want to ask in front of the group.

"Kellie. Kellie."

Kellie approached Amanda. "Hey, what's up?"

"Can we get a cup of coffee and talk?"

"Sure. Why don't we go to Crisper's?"

When they arrived, they bought their drinks and sat in a booth at the back of the restaurant. Amanda drank amount half her drink before she started to talk.

"Thanks for inviting me to the meeting." Amanda stopped. She did not want to offend Kellie in any way.

"I was uncomfortable when the Leader discussed…"

"I understand more than you realize."

Amanda whispered, "But it's murder. Besides, the women would never get away with it."

Kellie pondered over how much she should share. After all, Amanda was a DA. Finally, she said, "I'm not going to discuss the merits of what's morally right or wrong. In addition, when you walk in my shoes or some of the other women's shoes then we can talk."

"You're probably right but you didn't answer my question."

"Let's say that there are certain holistic compounds that don't show up in an autopsy."

"Like what?"

"I've already said too much. But remember, what will you do when your husband is suffering and he says he can no longer stand the pain and wants to die?"

Amanda appreciated Kellie for taking the time to talk to her and for being honest. However, the meeting and discussing her concerns with Kellie had left Amanda emotionally drained. The discussions were exhausting and for the first in her life, she doubted some of her beliefs and was questioning what she would do if Woody appealed to her to end his life?

CHAPTER 52

When Kellie volunteered at the Leesburg hospital she was privy to many conversations. Since Roger had been placed at Regal Care, she had eavesdropped on a variety of private conversations and prayers.

Although Roger had requested to be placed on life support, she knew in reality he didn't want to live as a vegetable. It was not a surprise to her that someone could take matters into their own hands and assist individuals to their death.

She recalled the time when she had passed by a woman's room and was stopped by the outspoken prayer.

"Dear God, I'm tired. Please relieve me of my pain. I'm tired of living. I know suicide is wrong, but I'm not sure how much longer I can live like this. In addition, I feel guilty when my husband and children come to visit me. My husband has no life and he seems so unhappy. There is nothing I can do, but I know if I were to die, their lives would be so much better without me. Amen."

That was proof to Kellie that some people wanted to die rather than live an unproductive life.

###

The dating service had a problem with the lack of deaths that had occurred. Kellie believed she had a possible solution to their problem. Diane and Arlene might support her idea, but Lisa would be a hard sell.

After Kellie stopped volunteering at the hospital, no one bothered to block her access to the hospital record database. Until the business ran into a problem, she had forgotten about it.

To help solve their problem, they would begin by accessing the hospital records. She wondered why she never thought about it before.

Not everyone puts an obituary in the newspaper when someone dies. However, all hospital deaths are recorded, along with the next of kin contact information. The hospital records would provide them with the identity of those women leaving behind surviving husbands.

In addition, if deaths still were not happening fast enough, maybe they could act as God's assistants. After all, if people are praying that they no longer want to suffer, why not answer their prayers. She didn't see the harm of assisting God in his work.

The problem was presenting her solution to her business partners. In some ways, her idea sounded criminal. But when you debated the merits of death and that it was going to happen anyway, where was the criminality aspect?

It could be done easily and no evidence of a crime. One day without the woman's knowledge, she would be relieved of her pain and suffering.

If no one approved of her first idea then she would propose her backup plan. It involved finding homeless men. They could visit or volunteer at soup kitchens or shelters to identify potential men.

Under normal circumstances, most women would probably turn their noses up at these men. However, with a bath, the right clothes, some money, and a job, who knows? Most homeless are people who happened to run into some bad luck.

She could remember before she married Roger how she could have easily been one payday from being homeless.

CHAPTER 53

The more Lisa thought about The Casserole Delivery Service, the more anxious she became. She wanted Diane and Arlene to support her. At this point, she and Kellie were as distant as if they were living in another country.

Lisa had to persuade Diane and Arlene to understand why the business had to be dissolved. It was going to be difficult convincing them to go against Kellie. The longer the dating service was in business, the more problems they were beginning to encounter. Lisa's primary concern was to ensure that no one got hurt.

No morning meeting was scheduled, but Lisa showed up on Diane's front doorstep. She rang the doorbell.

"Good morning. Did you forget we're not having a meeting?"

"I know. Can I come in?"

Before Diane responded to Lisa' question, she turned and left Lisa standing at the door. She ran to the bathroom.

Lisa stepped inside and yelled. "Diane. Diane. Are you okay?"

Diane emerged from the bathroom. "I'm sorry. I..." Diane couldn't finish her sentence as she fought to keep the tears from falling.

"What's wrong?"

Wiping the tears away, Diane walked to the kitchen. She wanted to discuss her pregnancy, but she couldn't handle the criticism.

"Would you like some hot tea?" Diane filled the teakettle with water and placed it on the stove.

"Tea would be nice but why don't you sit down and I'll do it."

"I'm..."

Again, without warning, Diane started crying, uncontrollably. Lisa went to Diane's side. Lisa put her arms around Diane and tried to calm her. After several minutes of loud sobbing, Diane finally relaxed.

The whistling teakettle broke their embrace. Lisa urged Diane to sit down while she fixed the tea. Lisa carried the cups to the table and joined her.

In a soft tone, Lisa asked, "What's going on?"

Diane concentrated on her tea. She was too embarrassed to look at Lisa. In a low voice, she managed to answer her.

"I'm pregnant."

Staggered, Lisa spit out her tea. She didn't want to upset Diane but she had to ask again. "What did you say?"

"Please, don't make me say it again."

Lisa was beyond shock. Not knowing what to do, she stood up and dialed Arlene's phone number.

"Hi Arlene. It's Lisa. Please come over to Diane's now." Hanging up the phone, she dialed Kellie's number.

"Kellie, it's Lisa. Come over to Diane's house. It's an emergency."

By the time she hung up the phone, the doorbell was ringing. Lisa answered it. Arlene was the first to arrive.

Arlene whispered. "What's going on?"

"Please sit with Diane. Kellie's on her way over."

As Lisa watched Arlene join Diane, the doorbell rang again. Lisa opened the door and Kellie bounced in.

"Hey. What's up?"

CHAPTER 54

Lisa took a slow, deep breath as a calming mechanism. "Ladies, I'm sorry if I sounded dramatic, but Diane needs us." Lisa was speaking with authority as she proceeded.

"Do not ask a lot of questions, but Diane's pregnant."

Slowly, Arlene and Kellie shook their heads, similar to when a dog is sprayed with water. Disbelief and shock covered their faces.

As Diane started to speak, her voice lacked confidence. It was barely above a whisper. "I was as surprised as you must be."

"Are you sure?" asked Arlene.

Through tears, Diane snapped. "Yes. I'm sure."

"I mean...at your age...I thought you were having menopausal symptoms. I mean tests do and can come up with odd results," said Arlene.

Wiping her nose, Diane responded, "Not in this case."

Arlene wanted to know. "Who's the father?"

Diane glared at her with disgust. "Who do you think? Sam, of course."

Throwing up her hands, Arlene gave an apologetic look. She went on to ask, "What does he think?"

In a low voice, Diane answered, "He doesn't know yet. I'm going to meet him tonight."

Lisa wanted to know. "How do you think he'll take the news?"

"Obviously, he's going to be surprised but I don't really know how he'll react."

"You're not going to have the baby are you?" Kellie said with conviction. Lisa and Arlene glowered at her.

Kellie shrugged. "You do have options."

"I haven't even thought about alternatives," Diane shot back to Kellie.

"Well, for God's sake, you need to. I mean, you're single, retired, on a fixed income, and you have grown children."

Lisa thought she would defuse this before the discussion got out of hand. Kellie raising her voice at Diane was not being helpful. Kellie was reacting more like a parent who had been told that her teenaged daughter was pregnant.

Making her voice as comforting as possible, Lisa began. "Listen, Diane. We will support what ever decision you make. However, Kellie does have a point that you need to consider all your options. I mean you don't have to have the baby."

Sadly, Arlene added, "What about adoption? There are lots of couples who can't have babies and would welcome a newborn."

Diane tried to be flippant as she chuckled. "Or I can keep the baby and marry my baby's daddy."

Lisa, Arlene, and Kellie did not laugh at her attempt at humor. This was not a laughing matter.

"Look, I appreciate everything you've said to me. It's just that since I received the news from the doctor I have been driving myself crazy thinking about how my life will change." She was unable to control her emotions as the crying started again.

Lisa handed her a tissue. Quickly looking at Arlene and Kellie, Lisa shrugged. Softly, Lisa asked, "What can we do to help?"

"Until I talk to Sam, I guess there isn't much anyone can do."

"I agree with you. You have to talk to that boy. And, the sooner the better," Arlene said firmly.

Kellie started to say something, but then stopped. What would be the point of bringing up the "A" word? Apparently, no one wanted to hear that as an option. She wondered why? It certainly was a viable solution to her problems.

"Look, I don't want to be rude, but I think I have a hair appointment today." Arlene made the statement, but her face was asking the question.

"Arlene, I don't know, but I appreciate you coming over on such short notice. Please don't let me keep you from your appointment."

Arlene mumbled something inaudible. She stood up to leave.

Kellie said, "Wait up, Arlene. I should be going too. Diane, if you want to talk about more options, let me know." Kellie hoped Diane understood her hidden meaning when she emphasized, "more options."

"I guess I'll go too," added Lisa.

CHAPTER 55

Sam's apartment faced the parking lot. He peeped out the window as he watched for Diane's arrival. He was nervous.

The only thing that had been on his mind was Diane and what she had to tell him. For a split second Sam had turned from the window and missed Diane when she pulled into the parking lot.

Diane was anxious about telling Sam about the pregnancy. Her life, as well as his, would be turned upside down.

When she rang the doorbell, her hand was shaking. Taking a deep breath, she waited.

Within seconds, Sam opened the door. Their eyes met. The only thing running through her mind was how incredibly handsome he was. He smelled delicious enough to taste.

"Hi, Diane."

He had the urge to pull her into his arms. As much as Sam wanted to kiss her he didn't. He kept his hands to himself. He waited for her lead. He stepped aside so she could enter the apartment.

"Come in." He added, "You look lovely as always."

When she passed him, all he could notice was her slumped shoulders and forlorn face. Whatever was going on, she was distant.

For a moment, Diane was anxious. The walls seemed as if they were closing in and she didn't have enough air to breath. Awkwardly, they continued to stand, avoiding each other's eyes.

Finally Sam offered Diane a seat. They sat down on opposite ends of the sofa. Out of Sam's peripheral vision, he thought Diane's appearance was gaunt. She was about to cry as Sam noticed her quivering lower lip.

Impatience had consumed his entire body. He couldn't understand why she could not tell him what was wrong? When he thought about it, Diane was entirely too old for all the drama.

Wringing her hands in her lap, she steered clear of any type of eye contact with Sam. Finally when their eyes met, she blinked back the tears. Sniffing, she pulled a tissue from her purse and blew her nose.

She tried to relax as she closed her eyes. When she opened them, she spotted a photo that was hanging half way out of an opened envelope.

"Diane, what's wrong?"

She opened her mouth but nothing came forth. She closed her mouth and tried again to answer him. When the words started spilling from her mouth her voice was barely above a whisper. Sam moved closer to her in an effort to hear what she was muttering.

She cleared her throat. As she began to speak, her voice wasn't any louder than it was before. She peeped at him through teary eyes.

He had no idea what was wrong. What was she trying to say? Annoyed, he thought, *This is really beginning to rake my nerves!*

As he was about to ask if she was okay, he watched her pick up the envelope that was on the coffee table. She stared at the photo.

CHAPTER 56

Lisa's heart was slamming against her chest. She was having difficulty breathing. Somehow she uttered.

"Do you mind if I ask you a question? How do you know the woman in the picture?"

"That's my sister." Sam pointed. "The man standing next to her is my brother-in-law and their new baby boy."

Diane thought she was going to go into shock. Instead, she ran to Sam's bathroom and lost all the contents of her stomach. She must have stayed in the bathroom too long. At the door was soft knocking.

"Diane, are you okay?"

She wasn't okay. All she wanted to do was to leave. She could not believe how her life had become full of twists and turns. When was it going to stop? She couldn't believe this latest development.

The knocking started again. She couldn't stay in the bathroom forever. Finally, she answered him.

"I'm okay, Sam. Give me a minute. Please."

She splashed cold water on her face and composed herself. The discussion about the baby would have to wait. She wasn't sure what she was going to tell him? She owed him an explanation, but she had no idea where to begin.

When she opened the bathroom door, Sam was standing there. Closely looking at her, he thought Diane's appearance had taken on a green hue. He wondered if she had cancer or something. He wasn't sure he could handle losing another person so soon after the death of his wife.

"Sam, what I came to discuss with you, will have to wait. I'm sick."

"I can see that, but before you go can you tell me what does my sister have to do with all of this?"

"Uh…your sister?" Diane acted as though she didn't know what he was talking about.

"Yes, my sister. When you looked a the photo…"

"Oh, that. I thought I recognized the woman in the picture. Maybe, someone I had worked with when I lived in Maryland."

"Well, my sister lives in Maryland. It's possible you might know her."

Diane dismissed the conversation and lied. "I almost called to tell you I wasn't coming over because I had a temperature earlier and a sore throat. I think I'm coming down with a bug or something. When I saw the picture, my stomach began to churn and I had to threw up." She was rambling.

"I'm sorry, but I have to go home. I'm really sick."

She picked up her purse and was about to leave when Sam grabbed her hand. He turned her around and held her close. He wanted her to feel safe. Whatever was going on, he wanted to tell her that it would be okay. Desperately, he wanted to kiss her but he didn't dare. He eased his embrace and released her.

"Why don't I take you home?" Instead of waiting for her answer, he hurried on.

"You could pick your car up tomorrow?"

"Oh Sam, that's sweet, but I think I'll be okay. I'll call you as soon as I get home."

He started to protest, but he changed his mind. He watched her as she walked to the door. He didn't want her to leave, but how could he stop her?

Without any further discussion, she left. Once she was inside of her car, she let out a deafening scream.

CHAPTER 57

Roger's medical condition was showing no signs of improving. To keep Kellie's mind off of her problems, she focused her attention on the dating service problem. Her concern was convincing Diane and Arlene that the business could be salvaged. She called Diane.

"Hi, Diane. How are you doing?"

"Hi, Kellie. I'm fine. The question is how are you doing?"

Arlene and Lisa noted they had not seen Kellie lately. Diane had defended Kellie by saying she probably had been spending her time with Roger. Even when Diane said it she was confident that Kellie had been with Chris.

Diane was worried that she was seeing too much of him. Unfortunately, she had not had the opportunity to discuss it with her.

"Fine."

"How's Roger?"

"He's still in a coma and not communicating." Diane detected sharpness in Kellie's response.

Diane tried to be encouraging. "Don't give up on him. Many medical professionals believe that people in comas can hear and understand what's being said to them. You're not wasting time visiting, talking, and reading to Roger."

"Maybe."

Diane changed the subject. "Arlene and Lisa have been asking about you."

"How are they doing?"

"Busy as always. You know them, they try not to miss golfing, playing cards, happy hour, and line dancing."

"The reason why I called was to talk to you about the dating service. Are we doing any better with the database?"

"Not really. I think we're going to have to reconsider whether we can continue the business. Lisa might be right in shutting it down. We had a good run but—" Kellie interrupted her.

"I have an idea." Diane didn't have to ask what it was as Kellie rushed on.

"At all hospitals, databases are maintained on all patients."

"What does that have to do with our database?"

"Well, I have the ability to access the hospital database. We could review the patient list of married women who die and have surviving husbands. The database contains information about seriously ill women. We could find out the prognosis of her condition and how long she has to live."

"Is that illegal?"

"Well…it's a small technicality. Besides, what are we doing wrong? We're identifying sick and dead women who have husbands."

Diane didn't respond.

"In addition, when we identify women who are terminally ill and have only a few months to live, we could easily help end the pain and suffering."

Diane was glad she was on the telephone. Her mouth dropped open as she processed Kellie's alarming words. Diane questioned Kellie to make sure she had heard her correctly.

"What are you suggesting?"

She gushed, "You know—the angel of bereavement."

Again, Diane sat with her mouth opened wide. Kellie actually sounded excited about her solution. No way did Diane want to be a part of what she was suggesting. They would be serial killers.

"Diane are you there?"

"I am. I'm thinking."

Diane thought, *Lisa was right, the business had to close.*

"Listen, Kellie, have you discussed this with anyone else?"

"No. You're the first one to hear my idea. What do you think?"

"Well." Diane paused as she searched for the appropriate response. "It's definitely creative." Diane rushed on. "Can I change the subject?"

"Yes but I don't want to leave this subject until I know where you stand."

"Why don't I talk to Arlene about it and then we can discuss it further. How's that?"

"Okay. That will save me from having to talk to Arlene. Besides, you're better at talking to her than me. What did you want to talk about?"

"How's Chris?"

"He's wonderful. Why?"

"Kellie, do you think it's wise to see so much of him?"

Kellie responded heatedly. "Why?"

"Well, I'm just concerned. Roger needs you more than you think."

Kellie didn't want to hear this. She knew what Roger needed.

"Listen, Kellie, I love you, but people talk and I think you should be more discreet. That's all."

Kellie responded angrily. "Who are you to be giving me advice? If anything, you should resolve your problems and then let's talk."

CHAPTER 58

Rather than call Arlene, Diane rushed over to her house. What Kellie had discussed with her was so sensitive she wanted to tell Arlene in person.

Ringing the doorbell, Diane prayed Arlene was home. As Diane turned around, she heard the door open. Arlene's manner of dress indicated that either she was coming or going from playing golf.

"Hey, girlfriend. How are you doing?"

"I'm managing the best I can considering everything."

"Well, if you ask me which you did not, you look exhausted. Come on in. I was about to fix me a sandwich. Do you want one?"

"No. My appetite is all messed up. I'm experiencing morning sickness all times of the day. Do you have any ginger ale or something like that?"

Arlene offered, "I have ginger ale. What about some crackers?"

As Arlene put ice in a glass she saw the concerned look on Diane's face. She handed Diane the glass and can of soda.

"What's going on?"

"Kellie called me this morning. She was...." Diane stopped.

"Maybe, you better sit down before I tell you," urged Diane.

"Is it that bad?"

Arlene sat down at the table. As she took a bite out of her sandwich, she waited.

"Remember the problem with our database?"

"Yeah."

"Well, Kellie has a solution."

Arlene wiped her mouth with her napkin and said, "Well, that's good news, right?"

"Don't get too excited until you hear what the solution involves. Kellie has a two-prong plan. The first part may be workable. We could use the hospital's database to provide us with the names of recently deceased women with a surviving husband."

Diane took a sip of the soda. "The second part of the plan involves us obtaining the list of terminally ill married women with husbands. Since they're terminally ill, we could assist with...their husbands becoming widowers."

"You mean we would...." Arlene couldn't finish her sentence.

"You must have misunderstood her. Surely, she was joking right?"

"No she wasn't joking. The reason why she called me is that she was hoping I would support her. She figured that if I agreed then you would probably go along with the plan too."

"What did you tell her?" Worried lines formed across Arlene's forehead.

"I didn't give her an answer. I told her I would discuss it with you and then we would discuss it."

"Well, I'm not supporting that crazy idea. I mean what would Harold say?"

Diane heard what Arlene had said but she wondered why she had said that? Harold was dead.

"What about Lisa?"

"She doesn't think Lisa would go along with her idea."

"If we go along with her idea, what would we to do about Lisa? After all, she is a partner."

"I was afraid to ask."

CHAPTER 59

Looking out the window, Lisa noticed Diane walking over to Arlene's house. Hurriedly, she took a shower and dressed.

Ringing the doorbell, Lisa absently glanced over her shoulder. She knew it had only been a few seconds, but she was uncomfortable while she waited for Arlene to answer her door. The cause of her uneasiness was that she didn't want Kellie to see her. The door opened.

"Hi, Arlene."

"Hi, Lisa. Come on in." Arlene added, "Diane's here."

Lisa acted surprised. "Is she?"

When Lisa walked in, Diane greeted her. "Hey. What's up?"

"Nothing," Lisa lied. "What are you two up to?"

"We were chatting about everything and nothing. I hadn't seen Arlene in a few days and thought I would check up on her."

"Would you like something to drink?" asked Arlene.

"No. I'm fine." Lisa rushed on, not wanting to lose her courage. As you know, I did not want to start the dating service."

Diane answered, not letting Lisa finish. "Yes. We know and understand your position. We had no right in forcing you to do something you strongly disagreed with. In addition, Kellie shouldn't have threatened you. We should have supported you."

Arlene nodded her head in agreement.

Lisa was pleased but wondered what had suddenly caused the change in their attitude? As much as she wanted to know she didn't ask. She decided to listen.

"Diane...Arlene, you have no idea how much this means to me." Diane patted Lisa's hand.

"I believe you, Diane, when you say the dating service has a problem. What is it going to take to convince Kellie?" Lisa asked.

"I don't know."

"Well, I think we should match the women we currently have in the database and take on no new clients. I'm really feeling uncomfortable with the...."

"I agree with you but Kellie believes she has a solution."

"Do you know what the solution is?"

Diane didn't dare look at Arlene. "No. She hasn't confided in me," Diane lied. "Did she tell you, Arlene?"

Arlene couldn't make eye contact with Lisa as she answered as truthful as possible. "No. I haven't spoken to Kellie."

Lisa tried a different approach. "What do you two think we should do?"

Diane answered for she and Arlene. "We agree that we should dissolve the dating service."

Lisa changed the subject and focused her attention on Diane. "How are you feeling?"

"Physically, I'm fine, Lisa. Mentally, I'm a basket case."

"How did Sam take the news about the baby?"

"I didn't exactly tell him." Diane chewed the inside of her cheek.

"What? I thought you were going to tell him?"

"I was, but it's complicated."

Lisa was concerned. "How much longer are you going to wait?"

"Not much longer. I have to figure out what I'm going to say to him." Diane looked away from Lisa's suspicious eyes.

"It's none of my business but..." Lisa wasn't sure she should continue. "Diane, you know I love you but time is of the essence and you have to discuss the baby with him soon."

"Baby!" Arlene said loudly. "Who's having a baby?" Diane and Lisa looked at Arlene.

As Arlene emphasized each word, her voice grew irritated. "Who's—having—a—baby?"

In a soothing tone, Diane replied, "Don't you remember me telling you that I'm having a baby?"

Diane waited to see if what she said registered with Arlene. Diane waited for her to make some sort of acknowledgement.

With sad eyes but a confused expression, Arlene answered. "I sort of remember."

Diane continued to respond to Arlene in a soft, comforting voice. "It's okay." Then she turned her attention back to Lisa.

"I know I have to talk to Sam."

"Do it today!"

Curious, Lisa asked, "Have you told your children yet?"

"I haven't said anything to them and I won't until I decide what I'm going to do."

"Well, whatever decision you make, I'm here for you," Lisa reassured her.

Arlene added, "Whatever you need, I'm here for you too."

CHAPTER 60

Lisa decided it was time to talk to Arlene's daughter. Arlene had given each of them her number in case of an emergency.

Arlene's daughter's had been named after her mother. However, Arlene nicknamed her Missy.

Although Missy had visited her mother, Lisa had never met her. Finding Missy's number, she dialed it.

"Hello."

"Hi, Missy. This is Lisa Henderson. A friend and business partner of your mother's."

"Yes. I know who you are."

Missy didn't want to jump to conclusions but she hoped this call didn't have anything to do with her mother. "How are you?"

"I'm fine." Lisa didn't know how to proceed.

"Uh...have you talked to your mother recently?"

"I try to talk to her at least twice a week. It's hard between mom's busy schedule and the time difference but I manage. Why?"

"I'm asking because..." Lisa was choosing her words carefully. "Well, lately your mother has been somewhat forgetful."

Again, Lisa thought she was really making a mess of this telephone call. Since she met Arlene, she had always been a little forgetful.

"I know she can be…" Missy stopped.

She was trying to recall if she had noticed a difference in her mother's behavior. The only thing that came to mind was her mother's recent obsession of talking about her father as if he were still alive.

"Missy, are you still there?"

"Yes, Ma'am. I was thinking about my mother. I have to admit, there have been some change, but nothing that alarmed me. I thought some of her forgetfulness was due to her growing older. You know, the normal aging process."

"I can see how you might think that. I mean there are times when I go from one room to another and forget why I went to the other room. But with your mother I sense it might be more than a little forgetfulness."

"You really think so?"

"Uh…yeah. Lately, she hasn't been herself."

"Can you wait a minute? I want to consult my palm pilot regarding my schedule." Missy studied her calendar.

"Lisa?"

"Yes, I'm still here."

"Thanks for holding. I think I can visit my mother in about two weeks. Do you think that will be soon enough?"

Lisa hoped she had not given Missy reason to panic. "I think two weeks will be fine. In the meantime, Diane, Kellie, and I will take good care of your mom. If something changes before your planned trip, I promise I'll call you immediately."

"I really appreciate you calling me about my mother. That's one reason why I love my mother living there. She's made a lot of friends and you all take care of one another. Again, thanks."

CHAPTER 61

Diane was at her wits end and wanted to discuss her problem with someone. She couldn't remember a time when she had been so stressed.

Reluctantly, Diane called Lisa. She had no one else. Her voice was strained. "Can I come over?"

Although Diane had not talked about it, Lisa suspected that the pregnancy wasn't the problem as much as her mental state.

Lisa hesitated for a moment and then told her to come right over. Diane didn't indicate what she wanted to talk about. Since the day Lisa met Diane, her life had been in constant turmoil. Lisa wondered if she would ever find peace.

When Lisa answered the door, she gave Diane a big hug. Diane had dark circles under her eyes and her face was red and blotchy. Her appearance indicated that she had been crying.

"Why don't I fix us a cup of hot tea?" offered Lisa.

"That would be nice."

Lisa put the teakettle on. In the meantime, they talked about the weather, golf, and Lisa's sister who was in the hospital again.

Diane waited until Lisa sat down. She needed Lisa's full attention.

"I know you're probably wondering what's wrong." Diane paused. She took a deep breath. She willed herself not to cry. Lately, that's all she did. She took a sip of tea as she focused.

"You're not going to believe what I discovered." She closed her eyes and said. "Joanne is Sam's sister."

Wide eyed and stunned, Lisa closed her opened mouth. "You mean your ex-husband's wife is Sam's sister?"

"Yes."

Before Diane could say anything else, Lisa shook her head and through pursed lips asked. "Are you sure?"

"There's no mistake. I asked Sam and he told me who she was. His sister sent him a picture of her, Fred, and the new baby boy."

"Did you tell Sam?"

"No. That was why I didn't tell him about the baby. I was distraught and seeing the picture I became physically sick. I mean I started throwing up and then…"

"Oh, Diane. I'm sorry."

"Can you imagine what Sam's reaction would have been?"

"No. I can't. Girl, your life has more twists and turns than the daily soap operas."

"You're telling me. Constantly, I tell myself that life has challenges and that nothing else could possibly happen. Then without warning something unbelievable turns my life upside down again."

"I wish I could do something to make it better. What are you going to do?"

"I don't know." Diane's eyes started to tear up.

Lisa hugged her and said, "I'll be sure to say a prayer for you."

"Thank you. I need all the prayers I can get. One thing for sure, I'm running out of time and I have to tell Sam about the baby."

"Are you going to mention anything about knowing his sister?"

"Not right now. We have enough to deal with."

CHAPTER 62

Since talking to Lisa, Diane's confidence had been boosted. Apprehensively, she dialed Sam's number.

Deliberately, Diane was calling in the middle of the day. To leave Sam a message was easier than talking to him. She had written down what she was going to say when the answering machine picked up.

Why was she afraid to face her problems? After all, she was a grown woman, divorced with adult children, but yet she was acting like an adolescent.

Diane was startled as she heard Sam's voice instead of the answering machine. She was stammering. "Hi...hi, Sam."

"Hi, Diane." Sam thought how her voice sounded like sweet music. "Are you feeling better?"

"Sort of." She had planned to take the coward's way out but now she had to talk to him. She wanted to know why he was home instead of being at work? She should ask him, but she had to stay focused.

"Listen, I was wondering if we could meet?" Quickly she added, "What are you doing later?"

"Nothing. Why, what do you have in mind?" His voice sounded sultry and sexy.

From the tone of his voice, Diane knew he was flirting. "I was thinking maybe you could stop by for dessert?"

"That sounds good. What time?"

"Say, seven o'clock."

"That's good. I'll see you later."

When she hung up. She let out a heavy sigh. At least she had made the first step. She had never been in such a predicament before and she wasn't handling it very well.

Diane was impatient as she paced the floor waiting for seven o'clock. It seemed as though the hands on the clock had stopped. When the time arrived and the doorbell rang, her body froze. All at once, it was as if every emotion hit her—anger, happiness, and dread.

Any other time, she would have been ecstatic about seeing Sam but today she was less than pleased. Taking a deep breath, she opened the door.

When she saw him, she began to melt as she gazed at an incredible, handsome looking man.

"Come in. You look fantastic."

"So do you." He reached out to touch her, but she pulled away.

"Please sit down."

He did as Diane asked. As he looked at her, he didn't like her facial expression—it was too serious.

"I'm going to get right to the point." She inhaled and then exhaled.

"I need for you to understand that I never planned…I mean, it just happened and I was completely taken back."

Diane had been talking too fast. When she stopped, Sam thought that nothing she had said made any sense.

"Would you please slow down?"

Diane began to cry. Between her loud sobs, he could not understand a single word. He wanted to hug and comfort her. He felt so helpless as he sat, watching her.

She blew her nose and tried again. "I'm sorry. There is no easy way of saying this. I went to the doctor for my annual check-up and…"

CHAPTER 63

Sam's body language was telling Diane that he was growing impatient as he watched her struggling to speak. Her body had begun to tremble. She prayed that an avalanche of tears would not start. She smiled ruefully. Swallowing hard, she made another attempt.

"From my symptoms, I thought I was at the beginning stages of menopause instead..." The words caught in her throat. "I'm pregnant."

"Did you say pregnant?"

Slowly, she nodded. With attitude, she added, "And please don't ask—you are the father."

"How did this happen?"

Diane laughed. That was the same thing she wanted to know. "I think it was the one time we had unprotected sex. That must have been the time when conception happened."

That sounded weird but she wanted to be selective in how she worded what she was saying. She did not want to sound as though she was placing blame on him. It was as much her fault as it was his. *Why was he looking at her as if he didn't understand?*

"You know...the time we didn't use a condom."

Sam leaned back on the sofa. His head was swirling as he pondered over what she had said. It was hard for him to comprehend that Diane was pregnant but that is exactly what she had said. He was going to be a father.

He thought he had been thinking to himself, but instead his words filled the room, like a skunk's odor.

"How could she be pregnant? How did she let this happen? I was under the impression that after a certain age, women were too old to conceive."

The minute he heard the words, he could not believe he had actually said them out loud. His intent was never to cause Diane the type of hurt that covered her face at that moment.

"I'm sorry. I didn't mean it the way it sounded."

"Oh you meant it. Please leave. Now!"

"I'm sorry. You know I love you. I would never do anything to hurt you. It's that I never expected to hear you say that you were pregnant."

Sam reached out to Diane but she pulled away. He could have kicked himself. How could he have been so heartless?

His behavior was no different than a high school teenager. He laughed inward as he thought about a talk show where the men are brought on the show to prove the paternity of a child. Before the father received the information, his reactions were usually pitifully immature—denying fatherhood, making ignorant statements, and taking no responsibility. He had acted no differently.

Not only that, he had not even considered Diane's feelings. If he was shocked, he couldn't even imagine how she must have responded to the news.

Diane moved to the door and opened it. She wanted him to leave.

He stood firm. He had questions that he wanted answered. "Diane, I'm sorry. We have to talk about this. Have you thought about what you're going to do?" He couldn't believe he had said that. "I mean…"

"You don't have to worry. I thought you should know."

"Of course I should know and I would have been upset if you had not told me. But…"

Diane didn't want to discuss this any further. All she wanted was for him to leave. "How about if I call you in a few days and we can discuss this further. Okay?"

When Diane closed the door, she sobbed uncontrollably. Reality was—Sam wanted no parts of the decision regarding the baby.

CHAPTER 64

As Kellie and Chris spent more time together, she knew she wanted to share the rest of her life with him. Chris wasn't one to express his feelings openly. As a result, she had no idea how he felt about her. She had not brought up the subject and she was afraid to.

Putting on the finishing touches to her make-up, she heard the doorbell ring. When she opened the door, Chris had the biggest grin on his face.

"Hi, gorgeous."

Kellie blushed. She smiled and embraced him. Her kiss was deep and passionate. Chris pulled back and looked at her.

"You need to behave yourself, young lady, or you're going to have to satisfy my hunger in more than one way."

Bashfully, she smiled. She took his hand and led him to the sofa.

"Would you like a glass of wine?"

"That would be nice."

Kellie poured the wine into the glasses. Chris looked fabulous. As far as she was concerned, they didn't have to go out to dinner. She wouldn't mind if they ordered a pizza or she could fix them a salad. Handing him the glass, she thought she might make the suggestion.

"Thanks." He took a sip and set the glass down.

He took Kellie's hand and stroked it tenderly. Kellie thought he seemed nervous as he began to speak.

"Kellie, I'm not going to make a lot of small talk regarding my feelings because that's not who I am."

"Since I've met you, you've made me happier than I can remember. In fact, I can't recall a time when I've been so content." He smiled.

"Kellie, I know we haven't been seeing each other that long, but I want to marry you."

Stunned, Kellie gulped. She never imagined he would ask her to marry him. On several occasions, he indicated that he was not interested in a long-term relationship with one woman. In fact, he had told her that he was dating other women. Therefore, she had accepted their relationship for what it was.

"Chris, you have no idea how flattered I am and under different circumstances I would probably accept your proposal in a heart beat, but I can't."

"And I know why?"

"What do you mean?"

"I haven't been totally honest with you. I never date anyone without having a full background investigation conducted. You were no exception. I know about your husband being in Regal Care."

He waited for Kellie to say something, but she sat, with her hands folded in her lap. She lowered her head, not wanting to make eye contact.

He continued, "Kellie, listen to me. I'm a wealthy man and I always like to know who I'm dating, especially if I'm interested in the woman."

As Kellie focused on him, she wondered if he knew about how she met him and about the business. She listened while he did all the talking.

"I don't have a right to ask you to marry me, because I know you're still married. When the day comes when you're available, I want you to be my wife. Will you marry me?"

Unable to say anything, Kellie sat in silence. Had she heard Chris correctly? He wanted to wait until she was available to marry him.

"Are you going to say anything?"

"But...it could be..."

Tears were clouding her vision. Then tears fell down her cheeks. She wiped them away with the back of her hand.

"I'm flattered, but you could be waiting a long time before I'm available."

"I don't think so." His voice was full of confidence.

"Now, will you marry me?"

"I don't know what to say."

"Just say yes."

Softly, Kellie said, "yes."

CHAPTER 65

When Diane entered her house, the answering machine was blinking. She listened to them. Twelve telephone messages and ten of them were from Sam.

Rather than wait any longer, she picked up the phone and returned his call. On the second ring, she heard his voice.

"Hi, Diane."

Diane hated caller ID. She did not own one but it seemed that more and more people did. People could see who was calling before they answered the phone. It was also a way for people to screen their phone calls.

"Hi, Sam. How are you doing?"

"Not well."

"I'm sorry to hear that." For the first time since she had been seeing Sam, Diane felt as though she was talking to a total stranger.

"Diane, I owe you an apology. In fact, I don't know how to convey to you exactly how sorry I am."

His voice sounded sincere but Diane had to protect herself. His reaction to her pregnancy was still fresh in her mind. When she needed him the most, he had abandoned her.

"I understand better than you know. Hearing the news that I was pregnant was not easy for me either. I have adult children who are married. I'm retired and on a fixed income. Not to mention I live in a retirement community that doesn't allow children under the age of nineteen to live here permanently."

"I know and I'm sorry. We need to talk. I don't want to do this over the phone. Can I come over?"

"That's not a good idea. Whatever you have to say, you can say to me now." Diane was not playing "pay back." It's that she needed to be in control.

"Besides, there really isn't much to discuss. I'm pregnant and certain decisions have to be made."

Sam was getting angry with Diane. Yes, he had acted terribly when she initially broke the news to him but now they needed to discuss their options. Despite what she thought, he did have a right in the decision about the baby.

"Diane, what do you want to do?"

"I haven't decided yet, but I do know I have options. I can keep the baby, adoption, or abortion." That was the first time Diane had included *abortion* as one of her options.

"How much longer do you have before you have to make your final decision?"

Diane was disappointed. Although she would not have considered marrying Sam, it would have been nice if he had offered. Not only that, not once had he said he would support whatever decision she made.

Then again, maybe she had been too blunt in emphasizing that *she* had decisions to make. Her heart was aching and her body was filled with hurt and loneliness. She tried holding back the tears, but they were running down her face.

Her voice cracked as she responded. "If you're asking, yes I still have time to have an abortion."

"If that is what you decide, will you tell me?"

In a low voice, she responded. "When I make up my mind as to what I'm going to do, I'll call you. Take care."

###

When the phone went dead, Sam sat and thought about his situation. Most women over the age of forty couldn't conceive, not to mention the fact they no longer had the need or desire to have children. He had dated lots of women and to his knowledge this was the first time he had ever gotten one pregnant.

Years ago, he had planned to have a vasectomy, but the day it was scheduled he cancelled due to the lack of guts. His male ego didn't want a doctor to possibly make one wrong snip and end his manhood. He was an intelligent man and knew the odds of that happening were unlikely.

Now, the only thing he could think about was what he should have done. But wishful thinking was not going to change his current situation. What was he going to do?

Even though he never had a child, his concern was Diane. Pregnancy at her age was risky and he would hate to lose her. He had to tell Diane about his fears and concerns about her having a baby.

Desperately, he wanted to talk to someone. He would love to talk to his sister, but since she had not been supportive about him dating Diane he could only imagine what she would think about the pregnancy.

He had no idea what he was going to do and he had no one to talk to.

CHAPTER 66

Lisa loved her family and she especially missed her sister, Rachel. At least twice a week, Lisa and Rachel called each other. When Rachel had been hospitalized, Lisa started calling her daily. Although Rachel was released from the hospital and recuperating at home, Lisa had not stopped calling her every day.

"Hi, Rachel."

"Hey, Lisa. What's up?"

"I have some wonderful news."

Rachel gushed. "You're moving back to Maryland."

Lisa mocked, "No, I'm not moving back to Maryland."

"Oh." Lisa detected a tinge of sadness in her voice.

"Remember me telling you that I was dating a man by the name of Patrick Baylor?"

"Uh…yeah, but you haven't said much about him lately."

"Are you sitting down?"

"Why?"

Lisa blurted out. "He asked me to marry him."

"Girl, you're joking."

"No. I'm quite serious. You'll love him. He's nothing like Paul, but he has some of the same qualities."

"Have you told Alicia?"

Lisa didn't answer right away. She had not told Alicia because she didn't want to have an argument with her. Ever since she moved to Florida that's all they seemed to do.

"No. I haven't told her. You're the first to know."

"When is the big day?"

"I haven't accepted his proposal yet."

"Why?"

"I have some things I have to straighten out and then I'll give him an answer."

"So, you're going to say yes."

Lisa couldn't tell her sister why she had not accepted Patrick's proposal or the fact that she may not be able to. Now that she was thinking about it, she shouldn't have called Rachel.

"I'm not sure yet."

"Lisa, what's wrong?"

"Nothing," she lied.

Rachel changed subjects. "Have you told Patrick yet?"

"What is there to tell?"

"You know what I'm talking about."

"I do but I don't believe…" She didn't finish.

"You have to tell Patrick if you decide to marry him. You can't start a marriage off with a lie."

"He knows who I am."

"Maybe he does but he doesn't know everything. You know what I'm talking about."

"No, I'm…"

Rachel interrupted Lisa and gently said, "I love you, Lisa, but there are times when I believe you're in denial. You need to tell Patrick or face possibly losing him."

CHAPTER 67

The words spoken by Rachel were not the first time Lisa had heard them. Her sister, Alicia, constantly told her to "be real."

She agreed with Rachel, Patrick had a right to know the truth about her. As Lisa considered her relationship with him, she knew it could not survive with lies and deceit.

Her biggest fear was losing him. She wondered if it was too late to tell him the truth? How would he react?

She knew Diane was consumed with her own problems but she wanted to talk to someone.

"Hi, Diane. It's Lisa. Are you busy?"

"Not really. What's up?"

"How are you feeling?"

"I'm okay, but from the sound of your voice, you didn't call to see how I'm doing."

Diane knew Lisa well enough that she could tell from the refection in her voice that something was seriously bothering her.

"Diane, I have a slight…" Lisa halted, not knowing how to continue.

"We're friends. If I could tell you about my pregnancy, you can tell me what's going on with you."

Stopping for a minute Diane joked. "Oh no. Don't tell me. You're pregnant too."

Diane started laughing. She was trying to make the moment light. Besides, unless Lisa was pregnant, as far as she was concerned, nothing could compare to that.

"No I'm not pregnant. I don't mean any disrespect, but if I were pregnant, we wouldn't be talking about it. I probably would have killed myself by now."

"No you wouldn't have. Now, what's going on?"

Without hesitating, Lisa asked, "What's my nationality?"

"Do you mean—what's your race?"

"Yes."

"I really never gave it much thought. I would guess, Italian or Hispanic. I don't know. Color isn't important to me. I'm more concerned about whether I like a person or not. Why?"

Her voice became soft as she said, "What would you say if I said I was African American?"

"You mean you're black?"

Diane didn't want to sound surprised, especially after she told Lisa she didn't care about such things. However, she was taken back. To Diane, Lisa's facial appearance—straight nose, olive skin, and naturally curly hair—gave her the appearance of not being black.

"Yes. I'm black."

"Well, you don't look black…I mean…what difference does it make?"

"Because my sisters think I should tell people, especially Patrick."

"Are you telling me he doesn't know? You didn't tell him?"

"What was I supposed to say?"

Diane didn't respond immediately as she thought about what Lisa said. How do you tell someone about your race?

Diane thought selfishly, *I'm glad that someone else has a problem besides me.*

CHAPTER 68

Roger was no longer in a coma. At night, it was the scariest for him. Things had changed since Kellie first placed him in Regal Care.

Everything had changed including Kellie. At least once a week, she used to spend the night with him. He couldn't remember the last time she had stayed. He could have asked her but the rejection would have been too painful.

Kellie was different, pre-occupied. He couldn't explain it. She visited him but her heart wasn't in it. She was merely going through the motions.

And there was the clear liquid she kept giving him. He wasn't dead yet so maybe it was one of her holistic concoctions she had brewed up in an effort to help him feel better.

He didn't know why he was paranoid about Kellie? When he had his first stroke, she was diligent about researching the Internet for information regarding stroke, recovery, and rehabilitation treatments. Maybe it had to do with her placing him in Regal Care opposed to him being at home.

The only saving grace was his visits from Lisa and Reverend Williams. They made him forget that he had a stroke and wasn't able to speak clearly. Lisa was extremely patient and encouraged him to talk.

He tried to tell everyone that something was wrong at Regal Care but no one understood. At night, Regal Care had a different personality. It was eerie when the lights were turned off. Besides the shadowy images that seemed to be lurking outside his door, there were sounds that made his hair stand on edge.

People were dying and no one seemed to care. He was encouraged when the police were called. An investigation was launched but nothing had changed because deaths were still occurring.

###

During the day, Roger slept. At night, he may have taken an occasional catnap but primarily he stayed awake. He didn't know if that would keep him alive but he wanted to be alert in case someone attempted to harm him.

It was almost midnight and he could barely keep his eyes open. It was as if he had been drugged.

###

By the time the first rounds were made by the nursing staff, most of Regal Care residents were sleeping, including Roger. No matter what he tried, his body gave in to the quietness of the night and to sleep.

Was he dreaming or was someone tugging at his sleeve. He didn't recognize the voice but it sounded female.

"Mr. Olson. Mr. Olson."

Slowly, he opened his eyes. It was dark. He couldn't see anything but an unnatural shadow.

The voice whispered. "It's time to cross over into the light."

CHAPTER 69

It was early and Diane had not gotten out of bed yet. She wondered who would be calling her. Usually, early morning and late night calls meant one thing—bad news was being delivered. She glanced at caller ID. It wasn't a long distance number so the call wasn't about her children.

"Hello."

"Hello. May I speak to Mrs. Diane Benson?"

"You're speaking to her."

"Mrs. Benson, this is the Regal Care Assistant Living Complex. Your name is listed as the person we should contact in the case of an emergency."

"Is something wrong with Mr. Olson?"

"Yes. Do you know how to contact Mrs. Olson?"

Diane was confused. Where was Kellie?

"Mrs. Benson?"

"I'm sorry. Have you called her cell phone?"

"Let me see. Can you hold on for a minute?" Silence invaded the phone and Diane waited.

"Mrs. Benson. Mrs. Olson didn't list that number as an alternative."

"Okay. I'll try to contact her. Do you want her to call or what?"

"Could you please tell her to come to Regal Care as soon as possible."

"I will."

When Diane hung up the phone, her head was swirling with nothing but questions. Where was Kellie? Why was she being cavalier about her responsibilities regarding Roger? Kellie expressed how much she was in love with Chris but Roger was her husband.

Counting to ten, Diane dialed Kellie's cell phone. Instead of Kellie picking up, Diane heard the answering machine.

"Kellie. This is Diane. Please call me as soon as possible. It's urgent."

Diane was angry with Kellie. If she had been her teenaged daughter, she would be grounded. Diane didn't know what else to do. She thought about calling Arlene or Lisa but what could they do?

An idea gave Diane a spark of hope. Most residents of The Villages listed their telephone number and address in The Villages phone book. She retrieved the book and thumbed through it. She found no listing for Christopher Franklin.

Now what? She had run out of ideas. Wait, the dating service had Chris's—no they didn't have telephone numbers, only addresses.

As she was about to call Regal Care, her phone started ringing.

"Hey Diane." Kellie's voice was cheery. "What's up?"

It took everything Diane had not to yell. Through gritted teeth, she responded. "Kellie, Regal Care called me. It's urgent. They want you to come as soon as possible."

Diane heard Kellie gasp.

"What happened? Is Roger okay?"

Diane could no longer hide her anger. "I don't know. Since Regal Care called me instead of you, I can only assume Roger must be in critical condition."

Diane softened her voice and added. "Kellie, do you want me to meet you at Regal Care?"

"Uh…no. I'm okay."

"Call me if you need anything. I'll be here."

CHAPTER 70

When Kellie hung up the phone, she was shivering. She knew Roger wasn't doing well. She should have been available. She placed Diane in an awkward position and she could tell from her tone that she was annoyed with her.

Chris was watching her closely. When Kellie's tears started flowing, he stood up and embraced her.

Gently, he consoled her as he asked, "What's wrong?"

Sniffing, she said, "It's Roger. I'm needed at Regal Care. They called Diane because they couldn't reach me."

"Listen, you did nothing wrong. Is he dead?"

"I don't think so. Diane said that I was needed at Regal Care."

"As I said before, you haven't done anything wrong."

Kellie didn't want to debate the merits of her behavior. Roger was still her husband and she had acted terribly.

"I'll drive you."

"No. I have to go alone."

"I'm not going to let you drive. You're too upset. I'll drive you and drop you off. If you need me, call and I'll come back as soon as I can."

###

189

Rather than let Kellie out in front of Regal Care, Chris pulled into a parking space. He turned to Kellie and wanted to take her in his arms but considering where they were and her state of mind, he kept his hands to himself.

"Are you okay?"

Kellie wiped away a tear and through sobs she said, "I'm okay. I really should go."

Kellie bolted through the sliding glass doors. When she approached the front desk, she didn't see the usual staff.

"Excuse me, I'm Mrs. Olson. I received a call from Regal Care about my husband, Roger Olson."

The woman dressed in blue responded. "Mrs. Olson, we've been waiting for you. Follow me."

Hurriedly, Kellie walked behind the young woman who provided no additional information to her and she didn't ask any questions. While they walked, Kellie didn't recognize this part of the nursing home. The woman stopped in front of the room where Roger had been transferred.

The nurse glanced up and down the corridor as if she was looking for someone. Turning to Kellie, she spoke in a low tone. "Dr. Bernstein should be here shortly."

Kellie nodded her head to indicate she understood. As she entered the room she was not prepared to see Roger in such a weakened state. Tubes were everywhere and an oxygen tent was covering his entire upper body.

Sighing heavily, Kellie summoned up her inner strength to remain calm. Her legs were wobbly, her stomach was queasy, and she was lightheaded.

Glancing around the room, Kellie watched the nurse checking and pushing the buttons on the various machines monitoring Roger's condition. When the nurse finished, she picked up a chart and wrote something on it.

"Mrs. Olson, I'll be back. The doctor should be here in a few minutes."

"Thank you."

Kellie moved closer to Roger. She kept her eye on the door as she leaned close to him and whispered.

"You're out of time. Look toward the light."

She sat down in the chair near the bed. Looking at Roger, Kellie thought his mouth was moving, as if he was trying to say something. His chest rose as he took a deep breath.

Without warning, the machines started beeping and making loud noises. A nurse charged into the room. Dr. Bernstein was behind her.

"Mrs. Olson, please step out the room."

Slowly Kellie backed out of the room. She remained in the hallway, pacing, wondering what was going on?

Finally, the door opened.

"Mrs. Olson. I'm sorry, but we did everything we could. Your husband's gone. Would you like to see him?"

Kellie tried to respond to Dr. Bernstein. The room was spinning as her body slid to the floor.

CHAPTER 71

At first Kellie was confused. Blinds were drawn but slivers of light were coming into the room. When she completely opened her eyes, she realized she must have been placed in one of Regal Care's room.

The room resembled a hospital room, equipped with a nurse's call button. She pushed the button. When the nurse entered the room, she was surprised but happy to see Emma.

"Hi, Mrs. Olson." She smiled. "How are you feeling?"

"I'm better. I guess the shock of hearing about my husband caused me to faint."

"We see it a lot. I speak for the staff when I say how sorry we are about Mr. Olson."

"Thank you. Please tell the staff how much I appreciate everything they did for my husband as well as for me."

"You're more than welcome."

"Am I free to go?"

"I think Dr. Bernstein wants to take a look at you before you leave."

Emma glanced around and lowered her voice. "It's sad enough when you lose a loved one but to add to your grief, a person shouldn't have to be subjected to questions and suspicion."

"What are you talking about?"

"You will be required to have an autopsy performed on Mr. Olson. In addition, you will probably be questioned about his death."

"I guess I don't understand."

Emma patted her hand. She whispered. "The recent deaths. There's still an investigation being conducted."

After Kellie was released, she walked outside to the far end of the building. The first call she made was to Chris. The second call was to Amanda Roberts.

"Hello, Amanda. This is Kellie Olson."

"Hi. How are you doing?"

Kellie took a deep breath. "I've been better." Kellie didn't want to cry as she added, "Roger died."

"I'm sorry. Is there anything I can do?"

"That's why I'm calling you. I may need a lawyer." Before Kellie could ask, Amanda answered her question.

"I won't be able to represent you."

"Why?"

"Because I'm a DA. If a crime has been committed, I would be the lawyer prosecuting you. But I'll call a colleague of mine and have him call you as soon as possible. I'm sure he'll represent you."

"Thanks, Amanda. I have to go."

"Wait! Kellie!"

"Yes."

"If the police question you, do not and I repeat—do not say anything until your lawyer is present."

CHAPTER 72

It had been hours. Diane couldn't understand why Kellie had not called. She was tempted to call her but thought she would wait to hear from her.

When Diane stepped into the shower she thought she heard the phone ringing. She turned off the water and listened. If it had been ringing, it stopped. As Diane dressed, the phone rang again.

"Hello."

"Diane, it's me—Kellie. I'm sorry I didn't call earlier but…" Her voice trailed off. "Roger died."

"Oh Kellie, I'm…what can I do?"

"Nothing. Listen, I have to go. I'll call you later. Please tell Arlene and Lisa about Roger."

Before Diane could ask any questions the phone went dead.

Diane knew she would have to face the wrath of Arlene but she didn't care. Besides this was an emergency.

The air was sticky and Diane's underarms were wet even though she had only walked a short distance to Arlene's house. As she approached Arlene's house, she saw the familiar note tacked to the front door.

Do not disturb. Knock or ring the doorbell at your own risk. Come back at eight o'clock.

Diane put her finger on the doorbell and held it there. Forcibly, the door swung open. Arlene's eyes were narrowed, her lips were pursed, and her hands were on her hips. She was madder than a baby crying to be fed.

"May I ask why the heck you're ringing my doorbell?"

Diane put as much syrup in her voice as she could without sounding phony. "Good morning, Arlene. Before you get upset, know that I love you."

"Whatever. But it's not a good morning because you interrupted my meditation. You know my schedule."

Pointing her finger to the door, she continued. "I know you read the sign." Crossly, Arlene waited for an answer.

"I'm truly sorry but that is an emergency?"

"No it isn't. Emergencies are usually taken care of despite what people think. If you had waited another hour I can guarantee, nothing would have changed. If you were bleeding, you would have called 911. Now, what's the emergency?"

Diane was irritated as she shot back at Arlene. "I said I was sorry that I disturbed you and you're right about emergencies."

Turning around, Diane stepped away from Arlene's door. As she started walking down the sidewalk, she heard Arlene's voice.

"Oh no you don't. My morning routine has already been interrupted. Tell me what's so important that you had a need to ring my doorbell so early?"

"Roger died."

Arlene staggered backward and her hand flew to her mouth. She guessed the news shouldn't have been a surprise but it was.

"What, when? How's Kellie?"

"I'll call you later."

"No you won't. Come on in while I fix us a cup of herbal tea. You can fill me in about the details."

Diane smiled to herself. Despite Arlene's tough morning exterior, she was one of the nicest, dependable women she knew.

While Diane was telling Arlene about Roger, she picked up the phone.

CHAPTER 73

Lisa was groggy and confused. Was her phone ringing? The feeling reminded her of times when she was younger and used to party and had too much to drink. The next morning she would end up with a hang over.

It had been after midnight before she fell asleep. The last thing she remembered was dreaming about Kellie. She was gushing about Chris and could not wait until she was a free woman and could marry him.

Slowly opening her eyes, she focused on the clock, reaching to turn the alarm off. It wasn't buzzing. The ringing was coming from the phone.

As she picked up the receiver, the answering machine clicked on at the same time.

"Hello. Lisa. Pick up."

Lisa recognized Arlene's voice. Lisa cleared her throat and answered. "Hello, Arlene. I'm here." She hoped Arlene did not hear the annoyance in her voice.

"What's so important that you had to call me so early in the morning?"

"You know I wouldn't have called if it wasn't urgent. You know how I am about my morning ritual?"

"Okay. Okay. I get it. What's so important?"

Arlene's tone was regretful. "It's about Kellie."

Slowly and deliberately Lisa asked, "What about her?"

"Roger died."

Hearing that, Lisa was wide-awake. That was the last thing she had expected to hear.

"What? When?"

"We think he might have died last night. Diane came over and told me."

"Have you talked to Kellie?"

"I haven't but Diane talked to her briefly. Diane received a call from Regal Care…"

Lisa cut Arlene off. "Did Regal Care tell Diane about Roger dying or Kellie?"

"No. Regal Care called when they couldn't find Kellie."

"Arlene, you're not making sense."

"Regal Care had Diane's name as the person to contact in case of an emergency." Before Lisa could ask any more questions, Arlene hurried on.

"Kellie called Diane and…" Arlene was talking but Lisa had tuned her out. Arlene had confused Lisa to the point there was no point in listening to her babbling.

"Why don't you come over to the house and join me and Diane?"

"Lisa! Lisa!"

"I'm sorry. What did you ask me?"

"I said you should come over to the house and Diane can better explain all the details surrounding Roger's death."

"Okay. Give me time to shower and dress."

"Are you okay?"

Lisa lied. "I was saying a quick prayer for Kellie. What Lisa was really thinking about was Patrick's proposal, Rosa, the business, and her secret.

CHAPTER 74

Quickly, Lisa showered and dressed. While heading to Arlene's house, she glanced at Kellie's house. Her car wasn't in the driveway.

When Arlene opened the door, Lisa's nose was assaulted with the most wonderful aroma.

"What is that smell?"

"Good morning, Lisa. I made a casserole." Arlene replied.

"Good, I'm starved. Diane, how are you doing?"

"Probably like you. Tired and trying to grasp the fact that Roger's dead."

Lisa answered, "Yeah. I guess I knew he was sick and any day he could die. The last time I visited him, he was holding his own."

"Yeah when I talked to Kellie, I had the impression that there had been no change," Arlene said as she poured hot water into cups, making tea. She peeped in the oven, checking on breakfast.

"Where is Kellie?" asked Lisa.

Diane shrugged. "I don't know. She hung up before I could ask any questions.

Arlene opened her mouth to say something but fell quiet.

For a moment, quietness filled the room as they sat blowing their steaming tea. Watching Diane and Arlene sipping their drinks, Lisa suggested, "We should go over to Kellie's house."

"We will but let's eat first."

While they ate the casserole, Lisa realized she didn't know that much about Kellie. "Diane, do you know if Kellie has any relatives in Florida?"

"I don't think so. She was an only child and I think her parents are deceased."

"What about Roger?"

"I think he was an only child too and they didn't have any children. Did you know that Roger had been married before?"

Lisa tried to recall. "If Kellie told me I've forgotten. Did he have any children by his first wife?"

"I don't think so," replied Diane.

Arlene interrupted. "Okay, ladies, now that we're all finished with our breakfast, we can visit Kellie. Let me grab my keys."

They walked across the street. Arlene reached Kellie's door first. She rang the doorbell. No one answered. Through the glass door side panel, Arlene peeped in.

"Kellie's not home."

They decided to drive to the nursing home. They had let Arlene drive and she got lost. She blamed it on the radio. The music had been playing too loudly.

Arlene made a U-turn around and within minutes she was pulling into the parking lot. Lisa glanced at the parked cars.

"I don't see Kellie's car. Does anyone else?"

"I don't see it, but her car could be parked on the other side of the building," Diane said.

Arlene stopped the car and unlocked the doors. They entered the main building through the sliding glass doors. They strolled over to the information desk.

"Good morning." They spoke in unison to the woman sitting behind the desk. On the pink smock, the badge denoted the word, "volunteer."

"Good morning, ladies. How can I help you?"

CHAPTER 75

Diane answered the volunteer. "We're friends of Kellie Olson. Her husband Roger died."

The woman responded. "That's right, Roger Olson passed away last night. His wife was here, but I think she left. I guess she either went home or she has gone to the funeral home to make arrangements."

In unison, they said, "Thank you." They walked out the sliding glass doors and back to Arlene's car.

Out in the parking lot, Lisa asked, talking to no one in particular. "I wonder where Kellie could be?"

Diane suggested, "That's a good question. I suggest we return home and wait."

"I would have thought she would have called one of us. It's not like she doesn't have our cell phone numbers." Annoyed, Arlene continued, "Did anyone call her cell phone?"

Diane answered, "I called her cell phone earlier, but she must have it turned off because her answering machine picked up. I left a message, but she hasn't called me back.

When Arlene pulled into the driveway, Lisa looked out the car window. Although no car was in the driveway, Kellie could be home. When Arlene stopped the car, everyone got out.

Arlene asked. "Do you all want to come in?"

"Only if you're going to feed me," Lisa stated because she had used up all her breakfast and she was ready to eat again.

"Come on in." Arlene checked her caller ID. There were no messages from Kellie.

"Oh my God. I just remembered I had my cell phone turned off. Maybe she called me." But when she checked her messages, the only person that had called her was Patrick.

Diane asked, "I wonder where Kellie could be? If she were at one of the funeral homes, it would take us forever to find which one. There's are too many to call."

Frustrated, Diane cursed under her breath. "She could call."

Arlene grilled hamburgers for lunch. She set up TV trays in the sunroom where they ate. Taking several bites from her hamburger, Lisa dabbed at her mouth. She wanted to bring up a delicate subject, but she didn't know how Diane and Arlene would react.

"Listen, since Kellie has been dating Chris..." Lisa did not know how to ask the question.

Arlene finished chewing and asked, "What are you trying to ask?"

"I guess I was wondering if she seemed like herself?"

Arlene commented. "If you mean, she seems happy, content, and enjoying life? Yeah. She's much different than before she placed Roger in Regal Care. Lets face it, Chris has a lot to do with her being content."

"I'm not going to say I understand Kellie's situation." Suddenly, Lisa realized Kellie no longer had a situation—Roger was dead.

Diane must have read Lisa's thoughts. "Roger is dead and now Kellie can do whatever she wants."

"You don't think Kellie could have..." Lisa changed her mind and didn't ask what was really on her mind.

CHAPTER 76

It was the unspoken words and the guilty glances that led Lisa to believe that Diane and Arlene knew something about Kellie that they were not sharing. She wondered why they wouldn't tell her?

"I'm going home. If you talk to Kellie, give her my condolences. Tell her I'll be praying for her."

In unison, Diane and Arlene answered. "We will."

Lisa slowed her steps and added. "Before I forget, will one of you please call me with the details regarding his funeral or memorial service?"

Diane offered. "I'll call you, Lisa."

When Lisa closed Arlene's front door, she spotted a car in Kellie's driveway. Lisa rang Arlene's doorbell.

Diane answered. "I thought you were going..." Before she completed her question, she noticed the parked car in Kellie's driveway.

"Kellie's home or should I say, someone's at her house because that's not her car. Can I come back in?"

"What's up, Lisa? I thought you were going home?" Arlene waited for an answer.

"I was until I saw the parked car in Kellie's driveway."

Arlene asked, "Whose car is it? Is it Christopher's car?"

"I don't know. It's not Chris's car."

Without thinking, Arlene picked up the phone and punched in Kellie's number. The phone was ringing. On the last ring, the answering machine picked up.

Aggravated, Arlene yelled. "Kellie, we know you're home. Pick up."

To Arlene's dismay, Kellie did not answer. She put the phone in the cradle. "I wonder what's going on?"

Lisa said, "You and Diane tell me."

Diane threw up her hands and glanced at Arlene. Arlene's expression was one of bewilderment. Before the discussion could continue, Arlene's phone rang. She looked at the caller ID, she whispered, "It's Kellie."

"Hi, Arlene."

"Hey, Kellie?" Kellie's voice sounded strained and barely audible..

"You don't sound like yourself."

"I'm tired. I'm sorry I haven't called before now but I've had lots of things to take care of and I had to be questioned by the police."

"What for?"

"Roger's death. Remember, Regal Care is still under investigation so every death is under suspicion." Kellie rushed on as if she had been talking about the weather. "Are Diane and Lisa with you?"

"Yes, they're here. They send their condolences. We've been worried about you."

"Thanks. I appreciate your concerns."

Arlene was disappointed. She was being vague giving brief information and she had said nothing about Roger's funeral arrangements. In addition, Diane and Lisa were staring at her with inquisitive looks. Arlene thought she would ask what Kellie had not volunteered.

"Have you made any decisions regarding Roger's funeral or memorial service?"

"Yes. I'm not having a funeral or memorial service. Since the police cleared his death, I can have his body cremated tomorrow."

Kellie paused as if to let Arlene digest the information. She rushed on. "I mean there isn't anyone who knows Roger here in Florida. And most of his friends and relatives from up north are dead."

"But don't you want…"

Kellie cut Arlene off. "I believe funeral and memorial services are for the living. I don't need the service to say my good-byes to him. I've already done that."

"Oh…oh…"

Arlene was stammering. She had no idea what to say. Kellie was calm and she wasn't the least bit emotional. When her Harold died she was a basket case but everyone handles death differently.

Kellie's voice was composed, almost without feeling. Although her decision sounded bizarre, Arlene didn't want to judge. Maybe what she's saying is true, but out of respect for Roger and his memory, Arlene thought she should have a service.

Arlene didn't know what else to say. "Would you like to talk to Diane?"

"No. I'm tired. Tell her I'll call her in the morning."

"Okay, I understand and I'm sure she will too. But I have an idea. Why don't you come over to my house in the morning? Say around nine o'clock. I'll fix breakfast for everyone."

"That sounds like a plan. I'll see you then." As Arlene was about to hang the phone up, she heard Kellie say earnestly.

"I love you all like sisters. I know I've been a disappointment at times but I've appreciated everything you've done for me. Always, remember that. Will you tell Diane and Lisa what I said?"

This was the first time since talking to her that Arlene heard Kellie sound despondent. "I'll tell them but is everything okay?"

"Yes. I'm just tired. Listen take care. Bye."

When Arlene hung up, Diane and Lisa blasted her with all types of questions. Arlene raised her hand to stop them.

"Look, Kellie is fine and the police cleared Roger's body so he's being cremated tomorrow. She's not having a funeral or memorial service for Roger."

In unison Diane and Lisa asked, "What?"

Lisa said, "What about the police?"

"I didn't understand and Kellie didn't give me time to ask her. Anyway, I don't know any more than what I've told you."

Diane asked, "Why isn't she having a service for Roger?"

"It doesn't make sense to me, but she said something about a service isn't necessary to say good-bye. Not to mention, he has no relatives or friends here in Florida."

Diane and Lisa were as puzzled as Arlene. They wanted to ask more questions but Arlene didn't know anything.

"I'm sure she'll answer all of our questions in the morning. She agreed to join us for breakfast."

CHAPTER 77

Every time Lisa closed her eyes, she saw Roger. His words were no longer slurred as he tried to tell her something. However, every time he began to talk, he would fall asleep.

Peeping at the clock on her bed stand, it read one o'clock. Tossing and turning, she could not believe she was wide-awake. The next day was going to be a long day and she needed her rest.

She started to get out of bed, but changed her mind. To help her fall asleep, she started counting sheep. It must have worked because the sound of her alarm clock was buzzing.

She turned it off. She read scripture and said a special prayer for Kellie. It was getting late. She wanted to arrive at Arlene's house early. She did not want to miss anything. Walking across the street, Diane was already standing at Arlene's door. They greeted each other as Arlene answered the door.

"Good morning, ladies. Come on in."

It smelled heavenly. The aroma was a blend of bacon, potatoes, onions, peppers, and cinnamon. Kellie had not yet arrived.

"I guess you all didn't see Kellie?"

Lisa offered. "I didn't see her. Plus, no cars were parked in her driveway."

"Do you want me to call her?" asked Diane.

Arlene said, "No. Let's give her five more minutes. After all, you all are a few minutes early."

At nine fifteen, Arlene told everyone to start eating and she would call Kellie. The phone rang four times and nothing. Arlene couldn't understand why Kellie's answering machine wasn't picking up.

Hanging up, Arlene dialed Kellie's cell phone. Again, there was no answer. The answering machine picked up. She left a message and hoped nothing was wrong.

"Ladies, ladies."

Lisa and Diane were so engrossed in eating and talking that they did not hear Arlene as she tried to get their attention. Turning off the television that was blaring, she tried again.

"Ladies." They looked up from their plates.

"I called Kellie's house and her cell phone to see what was keeping her. She's not responding to either phone. I left a message on her cell phone."

"Let's finish our breakfast and walk over to Kellie's house. I still have her house keys," said Diane.

They walked across the street. Diane suggested they look through the windows first before they use the key to go in. They walked around her house, peeped through the windows but couldn't see anything because the blinds were closed.

Standing back in front of her house, Lisa asked, "Diane, use the key and open the door?"

"Okay."

Slowly, Diane put the key in the door. She opened the door. Inside the foyer, she yelled. "Kellie. Kellie. Kellie, are you here?"

No answer. Diane, Arlene, and Lisa went inside. As they stood in the great room, they were shocked into stillness.

The room was empty. Slowly, Diane, Arlene, and Lisa went into the bedrooms. Again, they found emptiness. Either someone robbed Kellie or she had moved.

Lisa whispered, "Should we call the police?"

Diane answered back in a whispered tone. "I don't think so."

"Then what should we do?" asked Lisa, still whispering.

Arlene said, "I don't know but let's go. It's creepy in here."

As if afraid that someone would hear them, Diane, Arlene, and Lisa tiptoed out of Kellie's house. When they returned to Arlene's house, it took several minutes before anyone voiced an opinion.

Lisa stated with conviction. "I think we should call the police."

"Why?" Arlene wanted to know.

"Because something might have happened to Kellie?"

Diane asked, "Like what?"

Lisa shrugged. "I don't know."

"Then, why call the police?" Arlene asked then added, "I think it's a little premature to involve the police. What do you think Diane?"

"I have to agree with you. There's no reason to call the police. What could the police do? Besides, what would we say?"

"I disagree. I'm calling the police." As Lisa opened her cell phone to dial, she heard Diane yelling.

"Lisa, put the phone down." Their eyes locked. Diane lowered her voice and said, "Listen, if you call the police, what are you going to say?"

"Yeah, Lisa. What has Kellie done?"

Arlene's words stuck in mid-air. Lisa took advantage of what Arlene said.

"That's what I want to know?" Lisa raised her eyebrow.

"Lisa. Listen to yourself. Kellie hasn't done anything. Her husband died and maybe she moved. What's the crime?"

"None, unless she helped her husband to an early grave."

Arlene's mouth flew open. "That's what you think? She said the police had cleared Roger's body."

"That may be so but my intuition says, call the police."

Diane's eyes were narrowed and her voice sounded threatening. "I wouldn't do that if I were you."

Arlene supported Diane. "Kellie wouldn't hurt Roger."

The hairs on Lisa's arm stood on edge. She was lost for words. These were supposed to be her friends but at the moment she felt alone as well as threatened. "I'm going home."

When Lisa stood up to leave, Arlene warned her with emphasis. "Remember—no—police!"

CHAPTER 78

Something was nagging at Lisa's inner soul. As much as she loved her friends, she would not cover up a crime. The actions of Diane and Arlene confirmed her suspicions—they knew more than what they were saying.

Lisa wanted to call the police. She didn't have any evidence, but she had suspicions.

If she called the police, what would she tell them? Maybe, she would report that Kellie's house had been robbed. Maybe she could call the police anonymously.

She was so conflicted. She didn't know why, but she believed she was running out of time. She had to make a decision soon. Having no one else to talk to, she called Patrick.

"Hi, Patrick." Her voice was barely audible.

"Hi, Lisa. What's wrong?"

Before she could answer, she started crying. Through her sobs, she tried to tell him but she couldn't get the words out.

"Lisa, take a deep breath."

She tried to compose herself. However, something snapped her back to reality and she hung up the phone. She knew he was wondering what was going on but she didn't know where to begin. She had made such a mess of everything. "Lord, I need your help," she said aloud.

She decided to take a long hot bath and perhaps she could relax and clear her head. Getting out of the tub and while she was wiping off, she thought she heard the doorbell. She grabbed her robe. As she went to answer the door, the phone rang.

"Hello."

"Lisa, it's Patrick."

"Can you hold on for a minute? Someone's at my door."

When Lisa walked to the door, she looked through the peephole. She couldn't see anyone. She wondered who could have been at the door and left before she could answer it?

"Are you okay?"

Taking a deep breath, Lisa prayed she would not break into tears. She needed to talk to Patrick. After several minutes, Lisa started talking slowly.

"I have to talk to you in person."

"Okay. I can be there in about twenty minutes."

Quickly Lisa responded. "No. I'll come to your house."

"Okay, but, Lisa, I'm concerned about you driving and being so upset."

"I'm fine. I should be there shortly."

Lisa was about to hang up and added. "Patrick, I love you regardless of what happens."

Peeping out her window, she wondered if Diane and Arlene were watching her house. She was afraid if they saw her leaving, they would try and stop her. Backing away from the window, she chewed on her lower lip. How was she going to leave without them seeing her?

As she dressed, she came up with a plan. Walking, Lisa constantly glanced over her shoulder. Her heart was pounding excessively and every sound made her jump which prevented her from walking at a faster pace.

She was having a difficult time catching her breath. It seemed like hours for her to reach the Circle K gas station. When she did, she glanced over her shoulder before entering the mini-mart.

Sweat was cascading down Lisa's face. She pulled out her cell phone and called a taxi.

CHAPTER 79

Within fifteen minutes, Lisa was inside the taxi and using her cell phone. She alerted Patrick that she was on her way.

Impatiently, Patrick paced the floor while waiting for Lisa. He was more nervous than a man waiting for his wife to deliver a baby. At last, he spotted the taxi.

He ran to the door and opened it. Patrick helped her out the taxi. As the taxi pulled away from the curb, Patrick pulled her into his arms. They embraced, kissed and went inside.

"Lisa, what is going on? Before you arrived, I was worried half out of my mind."

"I'm sorry if I worried you, but Patrick its such a long story."

"We have all night. Do you want something to eat?"

"No. I've lost my appetite. But I will have a glass of wine."

While Patrick was pouring the wine in the glasses, he encouraged her to talk. "Why didn't you want me to come over to your house and why did you take a taxi?"

"My life was sort of threatened."

He almost spilled the wine. "What are you talking about?"

"I'll talk about that later. Right now, I want to stay focused. Let me start from the beginning."

Before Lisa started, she took a big gulp of the wine. "Rather than sugar coat what I have to say, I'm just going to spit everything out."

This time, she took a sip of wine. "When I met you, we did not meet by accident."

Patrick was puzzled. "What do you mean?"

"Well, being a widow for over five years, I was ready to meet men and date. I used a dating service, newspaper' ads, and the Internet."

His expression showed more confusion. "I didn't participate in any of those, so how does that affect me?"

"Please give me a chance to explain."

"I'm sorry. Go on."

"I wasn't having much luck using those venues so I came up with my own dating system." Lisa chewed the inside of mouth and decided this was not the time to mince her words.

"I found you by reading the newspaper obituary."

Patrick's eyes were wide. He cocked his head to the side and opened his mouth but said nothing. He closed his mouth and was bewildered.

Finally, he asked, "How did you find me by reading the obituary?"

"It's a little confusing, but let me try and explain. Every day I would read the obituary. I was looking for women who died and left behind a husband."

He interrupted Lisa. "In other words, our meeting was less than coincidental?"

"Right. I pretended to know your deceased wife in order to meet you."

Without warning Patrick slapped his leg and started laughing. Lisa wondered what was so funny?

"Lisa, I'm sorry but what's funny is that my wife was determined to find me a wife or a companion before she died. When she was in the hospital and suffering from complications from Diabetes, she tried to find me someone to replace her. She thought it was cruel for me to watch her die. She thought her death would be easier for me if I found someone."

It was Lisa's turn to be surprised. She listened to Patrick and thought that his wife had been an unbelievable woman. She must have loved him dearly.

"I never accepted her offer. In fact, I had no intention of getting involved with another woman when she died. You came along and I changed my mind."

Lisa exhaled noisily. "Since I'm bearing my soul, I have one last thing to tell you. It's about me."

"Before you tell me, I want you to know how sorry I am that you didn't feel confident enough to unburden your heart to me. I love you. I know this must have been tough keeping our meeting a secret. There isn't anything you can tell me that will change the way I feel about you. Do you understand that?"

Tears started to fill Lisa's eyes. *What did she do to deserve such a wonderful man?*

"I'm sorry too that I didn't tell you sooner. I hope you can forgive me?"

CHAPTER 80

Patrick kissed Lisa and held her tightly. He whispered in her ear. "There's nothing to forgive."

Gently, Lisa pulled away and gazed into his eyes. "There's more."

Blurting out, she said without hesitation. "I'm not who you think I am. I'm African American."

After telling him, she heard no laughter like when she told him how they met. He looked at her, but said nothing. From his facial expression, she guessed her sisters had been right. She didn't think the color of her skin would have made a difference.

"Lisa, believe me when I say I could care less about the color of your skin but I'm curious why you didn't tell me sooner?"

"What was I supposed to say?"

"What do you mean?"

Lisa said huffily. "At what point was I supposed to say—oh by the way I'm black?"

He didn't respond. When he thought about it, she made a good point.

"My problem is that I want people to accept me for Lisa, a woman and not Lisa, a black woman."

"I can't begin to say I understand how you feel, but I do know it must be difficult for you. I mean, I never gave your color a thought, but I can see why people probably think you're something other than black." He stopped.

"I mean...you don't look black..." He ran his fingers through his hair. "I'm not saying this very well. Anyway, I wouldn't care if you were black, brown, yellow, white, or red." He waited to see her reaction to what he had said. She said nothing as he continued.

"Lisa, I love you, but we can't have a relationship or a marriage with secrets and lies."

She nodded. "I agree with you but things got complicated." She started crying. He put his arms around her and kissed her deeply.

He wanted to make sure she understood that all was forgiven. "I love you. I hope you know you can tell me anything. Now, what else are you upset about?"

"Oh boy." Inhaling and then exhaling, Lisa began.

"I never wanted any part of the dating service, but Kellie threatened me since you didn't know how we met. I couldn't afford to have you hear it from someone other than me so I went along with starting the business."

"I understand that." He shrugged. "So what else? The dating service uses the obituaries to find the men for the database. As far as I know, you haven't broken any laws. I mean it's a little unconventional but I'm not sure everyone would be okay with your methods but so what?"

"Well, the business ran into a glitch. We were taking on too many clients. We didn't have enough men to meet the requests of our clients. No one would support me in dissolving the business." Lisa stopped to catch her breath.

"Kellie had a solution to our problem, but she never shared it with us. I should say, with me. I was not Kellie's favorite person. I'm digressing. Anyway, the next thing we know, Roger, Kellie's husband dies."

"But wasn't he, like ninety...."

Lisa chuckled. "No, he wasn't that old. He had suffered from a series of strokes."

"So what are you saying?"

"Now that I'm saying it, it sounds stupid, but I think Kellie might have killed him. I wouldn't be suspicious but since she's been dating Chris."

"Who's Chris?"

"A man she found through the dating service." Lisa was trying to patient but she couldn't understand why Patrick was having a difficult time keeping up with her explanation.

"She was dating while her husband was alive?" Patrick's voice reflected his surprise.

"Well, yes and she fell in love with Chris. That's why I think she might have killed Roger."

"Hold on. The only crime I see is that she committed adultery."

Lisa pursed her lips as she looked at Patrick. The last thing she wanted to do was to discuss moral issues with him. She wanted him to understand why Kellie might have killed Roger.

"Do you really believe she killed her husband? I mean what evidence do you have?"

"I have no evidence only my instinct." She could see Patrick did not agree with her conclusion about Kellie.

"Well, how do you explain the fact she's missing?"

"Whew. This is crazy. What do you mean she's missing?"

"Roger died and her house is completely empty."

"Maybe she moved."

"During the night—don't you find that to be a little unusual?"

"No, especially when you have nosy neighbors." He started laughing but stopped when he saw Lisa's serious facial expression.

"What do Diane and Arlene think?"

CHAPTER 81

Lisa shrugged. "Neither one of them are thinking straight. Diane has so many decisions to make about her pregnancy and Arlene, who knows what's going with her."

"Lisa, slow down. You have really confused me now. Did I hear you right about Diane?"

"Yes, she's pregnant."

"How did that happen?" He laughed. "I mean when did this happen? Is she okay?"

"She's known for some time. Under the circumstances, she's doing okay. But she hasn't decided whether or not she's going to have the baby."

"My...my." Patrick shook his head. "The dating service certainly has produced some interesting results."

"Patrick."

"I'm sorry. Kellie is missing and Diane is pregnant. What's wrong with Arlene?"

"Nothing, I hope. Her daughter is coming and will be taking her to the doctor. She seems to be having some memory problems. I suspect she might be in the early stages of dementia."

"I'm sorry to hear that about Arlene. But she's okay?"

"Most of the time."

"Now, getting back to Kellie. What do you want to do about her?"

"I suggested we call the police. That's when Diane and Arlene threatened…no they said with emphasis that I should not call the police. Not knowing what to do, I called you."

"I hate to tell you, but my head hurts. After listening to everything you just told me, I'm not sure I even understand it all or the ramifications." He paused for a minute and continued.

"If you call the police, exactly what would you say?"

"Since Kellie's house is empty, I was concerned that maybe she was robbed. I guess I was hoping they would lodge an investigation."

"You watch too many TV crime stories." He shook his head.

"I'm glad you're finding this amusing."

"It's not that. But you have to admit what you're concluding doesn't sound like murder. Do you want my opinion?" Lisa shrugged.

"Well, you're not going to like this, but I have to agree with Diane and Arlene. I think you're being premature in wanting to call the police. If anything, the police would probably think you're being a nosy neighbor."

He waited to see what she might say. She said nothing.

"I guess I'm the only one with a suspicious mind. Maybe, my imagination got away from me, especially with me dreaming about Roger. He's been asking me to help him."

"Oh brother." Lisa shot him a glaring look.

"I'm sorry. Can you leave this alone and let it work itself out? I mean I don't know how you jumped to such conclusions about Kellie?"

"Well, there were a rash of unexpected deaths at Regal Care. That's where Roger was living."

"And what does that have to do with Kellie?"

"I don't know."

"Let me ask you this, is Kellie having an autopsy done on Roger?"

"No, since the police cleared his body, she's having him cremated tomorrow."

"Well, there goes your case as well as your evidence."

"I feel like a fool."

"You're not a fool. I appreciate you telling me the truth and as far as Kellie is concerned, I suggest you leave it alone. I don't think that if you go to the police, you're going to get the results you want. Kellie's an adult. She's not missing until a relative files a report...." She interrupted Patrick.

"But no one would report her missing. According to Diane, Kellie and Roger have no relatives. Therefore, who's going to ask questions?"

"I guess no one. Detective Colombo Henderson, I think you're out of luck." Patrick had tried to make light of Lisa's concern but he could tell the wheels in her brain were still churning.

If a crime has been committed, no one will ever know."

"Maybe you're troubled because she didn't confide in her friends. With regard to her husband—well, he was old, had numerous strokes, and died of natural causes."

"Okay. Okay. Perhaps I did over react. I'm tired and going home."

"Can you call me a taxi?"

"No. I'm driving you home. I'll drop you off at the top of your street. If someone sees you, you can say you've been out walking."

CHAPTER 82

As time passed, Lisa began to accept the fact that Roger died from natural causes. In an attempt to relax, she treated herself to some pampering. She had a facial, massage, pedicure and manicure.

The only person she had seen was Patrick. She had not called Diane or Arlene and they had not called her.

Lisa had been grateful for Patrick's patience and understanding. Although he did not say it, Lisa thought he was worried about her.

###

It was early and Patrick hated to wake Lisa. Patiently, he waited for her to pick up the phone.

Drowsily, Lisa answered. "Hello."

"Good morning, beautiful. I'm sorry to wake you up but I have something important you'll want to hear. I know you haven't seen the morning newspaper because you're still in the bed. "

"Patrick, please."

"I'm sorry. An arrest was made at Regal Care regarding the possible homicides."

Lisa sat straight up in the bed. "What?"

"Yeah. A nurse named Emma Gordon. Did you ever see her when you visited Roger?"

"Yes. In fact, she was the head nurse in charge."

"Well, she was the one arrested. According to the newspaper article, she's also suspected of possibly murdering other patients when she worked at several other nursing homes."

"I would never have guessed it. I thought she was extremely nice, efficient, and caring."

"You never know, do you?"

"No you don't. This means Emma may have been a serial killer."

"If what they are saying is true, possibly."

Pangs of guilt consumed Lisa's body. She had been wrong about Kellie. She was glad she had not called the police.

"Lisa, are you okay?"

"I think so. It's that I feel guilty about the thoughts I had about Kellie. I call myself a Christian and I had no mercy regarding her situation. Because I abhorred her behavior, I wasn't understanding."

"I wouldn't beat myself up about it."

"But I was supposed to be her friend. I guess Roger died of natural causes but I wonder why I jumped to conclusions about Kellie possibly killing him?"

"I don't know."

"What else did the article say?"

"Nothing much. I bet if you turn on the TV, more will be reported on the early morning news."

"You're probably right. Now, that you woke me up, what about taking me to breakfast?"

Days after the arrest at Regal Care, Lisa still couldn't shake the haunting nightmares of Roger, asking for her help. In addition, Lisa had an unexplainable nagging sensation that said Roger was murdered. She admonished herself. She had to let it go. She had nothing to support her suspicions and she had to resign herself to the fact that Roger's death was natural. If he had been murdered, from what was being reported, Emma Gordon was guilty.

Except for seeing Patrick, Lisa had been staying in the house, mainly to avoid Arlene and Diane. She wasn't in the mood to talk to them, especially about Kellie, Roger's death, and the dating service.

In addition, they had not contacted her. Rather than act like an immature teenager, Patrick suggested she call them. After all, they were friends. She agreed to call them later on in the week.

In the meantime, Lisa was going to have a relaxing day by reading a book, watching some TV talk shows, and making some long distance telephone calls. While watching Oprah, the doorbell rang.

CHAPTER 83

Lisa peeped out the window. Diane and Arlene were at the door. Lisa opened it slightly.

"Hi. What's up?"

"You look like crap, said Diane.

"Thanks for that feedback."

Arlene added, "I'm sorry but I agree with Diane. You don't look like your usual perky self."

Lisa ignored the comments. What's going on with you two?"

"Can we come in?" Arlene asked.

Lisa hesitated. "Where were my manners?" Lisa's voice was less than sincere and opened the door to let them enter.

"Do you want something to drink?"

Lisa fixed three unsweetened ice teas and made a platter of cheese, crackers, and fruit. Putting the tray down, she wanted some answers.

"Have you heard from Kellie?"

In unison, they answered, "no."

"With Kellie missing, can we agree to dissolve the dating service?" Lisa looked at Diane and then Arlene. She waited for one of them to respond.

Arlene answered. "I have no problem dissolving the business."

"What about you, Diane?"

"Same with me. I don't think we have much of a choice." They had made Lisa's day but she wondered, *Why the visit?*

"Lisa, how are you doing? We haven't seen you. In addition, we wanted to apologize for telling you not to call the police about Kellie."

It was several minutes before Lisa accepted their apology. She wanted them to sweat. She had no clue what they knew about Kellie and the chances of her finding out were slim to none.

"Let's do something fun." Clapping her hands, Arlene sounded like a seven-year-old child.

"Let's start by going to dinner," suggested Arlene.

All of the recent events made Arlene seem like her old self again. Lisa thought maybe she had been premature in calling Arlene's daughter.

"I don't know, Arlene. I'm not in the mood for going out and..."

Arlene stomped her foot and said, "But I want to. Her voice sounded more juvenile than adult.

"Please. Pretty please."

Diane supported Arlene. "Oh come on, Lisa, we haven't been out in a long time."

They waited for Lisa's answer. Finally she responded. "Okay. What time do you want to go?"

"Say six o'clock."

"I'll drive," Lisa volunteered.

They met in front of Lisa's house. On the way to Beef O'Brady's, she stopped at the central postal office where they received their mail, picked up packages, mailed letters, and bought stamps. Everyone went to their individual mailboxes.

When they returned to Lisa's car, they each had a letter from Kellie. The postmark was Florida. Sitting in Lisa's car, they opened their letters. From the envelopes, the letters seemed identical.

CHAPTER 84

Diane volunteered to read her letter out loud. Lisa and Arlene would read their letters at the same time to see if she wrote the same thing to them. If their letter said something different, they would stop her.

Dear Diane,

I hope you're feeling better these days. I'm doing well. Words cannot describe how happy I am.

You probably already figured it out but "yes" I married Chris. It's not important where I am or why I moved without telling you. It's not that it's a secret but so much happened in such a short period of time that I needed time to figure things out.

I know you have lots of questions for me, but don't spend too much time trying to find answers to them. Things happen. Besides, sometimes you're better off not knowing the answers. I made certain decisions because that's what was best for me at the time.

I sent Arlene and Lisa a similar letter. The only difference is that I'm sending you information regarding the business. I'm enclosing a notarized document that legalizes the fact that I'm giving up my share of the business.

If I'm entitled to any profit, I want you to put the money in a college fund for your baby. If you decide not to have the baby then hold the check for me and I'll collect some day.

It was good while it lasted. I received more than I could have ever wished for, if you know what I mean. I pray that you will do what is best for you.

I look forward to the day when we see each other again. I wish you much happiness. I hope you can be as content as I am.

Love you more than a friend,
Kellie

When Diane finished, Arlene said. "My letter doesn't say anything about that notarized document."

Slowly, Diane said, "But does everything else read the same?"

Hesitantly, Arlene replied, "Well, I guess so."

Patiently, Diane said, "Then, you received the same letter."

They sat for a few minutes. Finally, Lisa put her letter back inside the envelope. She drove out of the parking lot. No one said anything.

When they arrived at Beef O'Brady, they were able to sit in a booth in the back of the restaurant. They placed their drink orders and everyone ordered chicken wings. It was happy hour and the wings were the special.

"What do you think about Kellie's letter? Do you think she knows about Emma Gordon?" Lisa asked as her eyes sparkled.

Arlene said. "I don't know."

"What do you think Diane?"

"About what?"

"Roger's death?"

"Nothing. He either died of natural causes or at the hand of Emma Gordon. We'll probably never know the truth."

Arlene ended the conversation about Roger's death. "You all will finally have a chance to meet my daughter, Missy. She's coming to visit me. In addition, she's requested a transfer to the Orlando office."

Lisa and Diane were ecstatic for Arlene. Lisa hoped she had not influenced Missy's decision. Arlene was definitely having medical problems, but Lisa didn't know to what extent and she didn't believe there was a reason to panic.

Diane updated them regarding her situation. "I finally talked to Sam. Everything has been decided. I have a doctor's appointment next week and he's going with me."

"Well…" Lisa looked inquisitively at Diane. Was that all the information she was going to share?

She must have read Lisa's mind. "If you're wondering what I'm doing…well, I'm having and keeping the baby."

"Is that what you want?" asked Arlene.

"Yeah, I think so. But if I change my mind, there's always adoption."

The three of them sat quietly. Lisa had other questions but she knew it wasn't the time or the place to ask them. She wanted to ask about Sam's sister, were they getting married, where would she be living?

Arlene was the one who broke the silence. "Who's Sam?"

Lisa glanced at Diane. Neither of them answered her. They should have, but they waited to see if she asked again. She didn't.

Lisa thought, *Thank God, Missy would be here soon.*

"Well, since we're playing catch up. Patrick proposed to me, but I haven't accepted yet."

"What are you waiting for?"

"Well, now that the business will be dissolved and I've told the truth about everything, I can accept his proposal."

Lisa winked at Diane and smiled. For a moment, she thought about telling Arlene but changed her mind.

In unison, they said, "Congratulations."

Diane said, "Well, I guess we won't be reading the obituaries or making any more casserole deliveries."

They all laughed.

228

Printed in the United States
83807LV00004B/1-75/A